THE WITCH'S SECRET LOVE

WITCHES OF BEFANA BAY

DEANNA CHASE

ABOUT THIS BOOK

Lily Easton is a witch who makes a living writing satire for an advice column in Befana Bay's weekly newspaper. Although she pretends to be jaded in love, it turns out, she's a romantic at heart. It's just too bad that she's fallen for Braxton Kirkwood, a man who's sworn off love. Frustrated by her lack of love prospects, Lily throws herself into work. But when half-a-dozen witches in Befana Bay start taking Lily's obviously bad advice, it soon becomes clear her pen is poisoned and is compelling the witches to stalk her favorite eligible bachelor, Braxton Kirkwood. Now she has to break the spell before they chase off the one man she's ever loved.

When it comes to love, Braxton Kirkwood is cursed. Literally. All it took was dating one crazy witch and now he's destined for every new relationship to implode before the third date. It's why he won't let himself date Lily Easton, even though she's already stole his heart with her sharp tongue and sweet smile. But when he suddenly finds himself being stalked by not just one witch, but six, he has to turn to the one witch he can't resist—Lily Easton.

CHAPTER 1

"I'M HERE!" Lily called as she hurried across the outdoor patio of The Salt Circle. "Don't order without me."

Sage Easton looked past the waiter and smirked at her youngest sister. "I knew that text about afternoon cocktails would light a fire under your feet."

Lily slipped into a chair across from Sage and smiled up at the waiter. After being trapped behind her computer for three days straight to meet a deadline, she was more than ready for an adult refreshment. What better place for lunch and a cocktail than the bayside café that was right in downtown Befana Bay? "Pomegranate martini, and don't skimp on the tini."

"She means vodka," Sage said. "Two please."

"He knew what I meant." Lily rolled her eyes at Sage and wondered if older sisters ever stopped being know-it-alls. She turned her attention to the handsome waiter and, not for the first time, wondered what it would be like to run her hands through his thick dark hair. "Right, Gavin?"

Gavin chuckled softly as he nodded. And then instead of writing down their order, he snapped his fingers and instantly two pomegranate martinis appeared on the table. "Those should have plenty of tini." He winked and added, "I'll be back in a minute to take your order."

"You should date him," Sage said with a knowing smile as he retreated. "I bet he wouldn't disappear after locking lips with you."

"No can do," Lily said, shaking her head sadly. "His birthday is in late July. You know how I feel about Leos. There can only be one peacock in a relationship."

Sage raised one questioning eyebrow. "What's Braxton's sign?"

Lily sighed heavily. "Sagittarius. The perfect fit for a Leo. Too bad he keeps kissing me and then bolting. I don't do mixed signals. If he's not man enough to actually ask me out on a date, then the hell with him. I'm not into games." Lily was still mad that the owner of The Enchanted Outdoors couldn't sack up and actually do something about their obvious attraction. "Besides. He stole that painting of August's from me. Not cool."

Sage let out a bark of laughter. "Stole? That's a little harsh, isn't it? All he did was buy one of August's paintings at the gallery opening. It's not like anyone knew you wanted it."

Lily ignored her sister's comment. In her mind, Braxton had snatched that sunrise painting of downtown right out of her hands. Who cared if it was an exaggeration? If it kept her mad at him, then that was a win in her book. Anything to keep from thinking about the kiss he'd laid on her when he'd followed her out of the gallery just before he'd bolted... again. The first time had been at the Witches Ball three months earlier, and frankly, Lily wished Braxton had never turned up in Befana Bay. He was proving to be a giant pain in her backside.

Her current plan of action was to just ignore him. She didn't have any real reason to go into The Enchanted Outdoors. She had all the outdoor equipment she needed. It seemed simple, right?

If only.

For some reason she couldn't seem to get that last kiss out of her mind. And she was starting to hate him for it.

"Whoa. What's that look?" Sage asked, her brows furrowed with concern. "You kinda look like you want to murder someone."

"That's a little extreme," Lily said, forcing a tight smile. "But I wouldn't mind if he suffered a boil or two."

"Evil," Sage said with a shake of her head. "But I can't say I blame you. If August had run so hot and cold on me when we were getting together, I'd have fed him to the orcas."

Lily snorted. "Good luck with that. I think they've adopted him into their pod." The man had an uncanny knack of being able to communicate with the majestic animals. She'd never seen anything like it.

"True. Maybe he'd have been crab food instead. Those claws are brutal." She smirked. "Anyway, enough of that." Sage pulled out the Befana Bay Bell and cleared her throat.

3

"Let's see what Endora has to say in the latest 'Ask Endora' column."

"Really?" Lily said with a groan. "Why do you torture me?" Lily had a feature in the local paper called "Ask Endora," and while it was a blast to write, she was always nervous when anyone talked about her satirical advice.

"Because," Sage said with a laugh. "This is gold." She cleared her throat. "Dear Endora, I've had my eye on a guy in town for almost two months now. He's friendly and we flirt every time I step into his establishment, but so far, he hasn't asked me out. I don't know how to make it any clearer that I'm interested. He's definitely single, so it's not that. Any advice on how to finally get that date with my rugged mountain man? Signed, Pining in Befana Bay."

"Stop." Lily covered her eyes with one hand. "You're not going to read what I wrote, are you?"

Sage snickered. "How can I not? I want to be a fly on the wall when Pining actually does this."

"It's satire, Sage. They aren't supposed to actually take my advice."

"They should. I don't know one man who wouldn't love this approach. August sure wouldn't have balked." She laughed and then continued reading the article. "Dear Pining, Any man who is so dense that he can't seal the deal for a date after endless flirting obviously needs to be knocked over the head with your intentions. I suggest you show up in a trench coat and your sexiest lace-up boots. Nothing else. Ask for help with a broken lace and once you have his full attention, flash him the goods."

"That's enough," Lily said, looking around and flushing

when she noticed the couple sitting next to them were staring with rapt attention at Sage.

"Oh, no." Sage shook her head. "The next paragraph is the best part." She grinned at the couple listening in and continued. "Once he's too shocked to speak, thank him for the invite to your favorite restaurant and tell him you'll meet him there at seven that evening. Then walk off before he has a chance to respond. No doubt, he'll be at that restaurant armed with flowers and condoms." Sage was laughing so hard she could barely get out the word *condom*. She wiped her eyes and finished the article. "Or, you know, maybe forgo the flashing and just ask him out. Both ways will unequivocally alert him to your interest."

"Oh, the trench coat is definitely the way to go." The older man who was sitting behind Sage gave them a solemn nod, and the couple started cackling.

Lily reached over and grabbed the paper from her sister. "Why do you always insist on embarrassing me?"

"I don't know why you think that's embarrassing. Everyone loves your column. It's amusing, and you're good at it. You should be proud."

"I am," Lily said quietly. "I just prefer to be a little more discreet about it."

Sage rolled her eyes. "Lily, the entire town knows you're the one who writes the column. It's not like it's a mystery."

"I know, but I just prefer to let the words shine instead of having the focus on me."

"Fair enough." Sage lifted her cocktail. "Here's to sister time on a Tuesday afternoon and taking time out of work to enjoy it."

Lily grinned at her sister, knowing this was a huge shift for Sage. She was such a workaholic that earlier in the year, their grandmother had actually taken Sage's power away so that she couldn't work. Her magically infused glass creations had been on hold until she'd learned a little work-life balance. And while Lily had thought her grandmother's tactics were a bit over the top, it had ended well for Sage. She'd found her partner, August, and had started taking time away from her studio and gallery at least once a week for cocktails and gossip with whichever sisters were available. It was a great start. "Thanks. Too bad Prim and Indigo couldn't make it today, but we'll drink their share."

Sage chuckled and clinked her glass. "I like the way you think."

After they'd finished their lunch, Lily followed her sister out of the restaurant.

"Want to come by the gallery to see my latest creation?" Sage asked, shielding her eyes from the summer sun.

"Sure. What is it?" Lily fell into step beside her sister as they started to walk up Witch Tower Road, away from the bay.

"A glowing chandelier. This one is jasmine vines, and the flowers light up with voice activation. I'm really excited about it."

"Dang, Sage. That sounds wonderful," Lily said wistfully. Sometimes she wished she had even half the talent her sister did when it came to making art. There was just something so satisfying about working with her hands. Too bad everything she tried to create ended up looking like a grade school craft project. Words had always been her strong suit.

"I think it could be. Needs a little tweaking, but with some refining, I think it could really be a showstopper." Sage radiated with pride, and Lily took her hand, squeezing it.

"I'm sure—" Lily started, but she stopped midsentence when she saw a tall, middle-aged, busty woman with bright red hair, wearing only lace-up boots and a trench coat so short that a glimpse of her butt cheeks was showing. The woman was striding straight for the front door of The Enchanted Outdoors. She had a fishing pole in one hand and her phone in the other.

"Whoa. That's quite a statement," Sage said as her gaze locked on the woman.

The door swung open and, as luck would have it, Braxton Kirkwood strode out onto the sidewalk with another customer and headed straight for the line-up of kayaks. The same Braxton Kirkwood she'd been trying to forget ever since the hit-and-run kiss at August's gallery opening.

"Braxton," the busty redhead said in a voice that nearly purred.

Braxton glanced over at her, and his welcome expression turned to one of complete confusion. "Cynthee? What—"

"My pole needs fixing," Cynthee said, thrusting it out toward him.

He tore his gaze from her barely covered body and focused on the fishing pole. "What's, uh…" He cleared his throat. "What's the problem?"

"It doesn't… um… the line is stuck, I think," she finished lamely.

"Okay, I'll just take a look and—"

Cynthee jerked the pole away from his reach and tossed it to the ground as she reached for the belt of her trench coat.

Three things happened at once. The hook at the end of the fishing pole latched onto the pocket of the trench and whipped one side open, jerking Cynthee and causing her to trip over the fishing pole. She went down hard with an *oomph*, one arm trapped under her body as she lay completely exposed on the sidewalk.

"Mommy!" a young boy called, pointing at Cynthee with wide eyes. "Why does she get to wear her birthday suit?" Before the child's mother could respond, the boy pulled his shirt off and started to strip off his trousers.

"Mikey, no!" the mother called, grabbing his shirt and running over to him.

Cynthee struggled to get up, and it quickly became apparent that the fishing line had gotten tangled around her boots, and she had no way to get to her feet until the line was cut. "Oh, no," Cynthee whimpered as she looked over at Braxton. "This didn't go as planned."

He raised his eyebrows so high Lily thought they might disappear behind his hairline. "You're... ah... I mean..." he waved a hand in her direction. "You need to cover up."

Mikey was standing over her, his shirt still off, but he'd managed to keep his trousers. "I'm Mikey," he said cheerfully.

Mikey's mom snatched him around the waist and covered his eyes as she scowled at Cynthee. "Put your clothes back on. What's wrong with you?"

Cynthee's eyes filled with tears as she struggled to close the trench, but she was laying on too much of it to fully cover herself.

Sage leaped into action, pulling a pocketknife out of the pocket of her jeans. She quickly went to work on the fishing line and then helped Cynthee to her feet before yanking the trench closed. She took a step back and studied the woman. "Were you just about to ask Braxton out?"

Cynthee's cheeks turned bright pink, confirming Sage's suspicions. But all she said was, "Sorry." She cast a quick horrified glance in Braxton's direction, and when she saw him scowling, she hung her head and hurried over to a red Kia that was parked just beyond The Enchanted Outdoors.

Sage turned to Lily and snickered. "Seems like she forgot the most important part of your advice. She forgot to thank Braxton for the dinner invitation."

"What?" Lily asked, turning to stare at her sister. She didn't really think that Cynthee had taken the day's satirical advice that seriously, did she?

"That scene had your words written all over it," Sage said with a chuckle. "Too bad she blundered it."

Lily couldn't help it. Laughter bubbled up from the back of her throat, and suddenly she was laughing so hard that tears rolled down her cheeks.

CHAPTER 2

BRAXTON STOOD ON THE SIDEWALK, staring at Lily Easton and seething. "You think this is funny?" he barked in her direction.

Lily instantly sobered and stood up straight to stare him in the eye. "Yes. Objectively, it is funny."

"I suppose you would think that since it's what you wrote in your article." Braxton turned to the lady who was still shielding her son's eyes. "I am so sorry, ma'am. That sort of behavior is not acceptable. I can't for the life of me understand why Cynthee would do something like that."

"You can't?" The woman scoffed. "Seemed pretty clear to me what she was looking for. Perhaps you should seek a better class of company." She took her son by the hand and tugged him away from Braxton's shop, lifting her head and sniffing the air with judgment as she went.

The man Braxton had been helping chuckled and said,

"I'll think about these kayaks and get back to you in a few days." He shook Braxton's hand and was still chuckling as he walked to his vehicle.

Lily hadn't moved and stood with her sister, a smirk on her face.

"What's that look for?" Braxton asked, irritated, but mostly at himself. Why was it that even now, when she was mocking him, all he wanted to do was grab her and kiss the smirk right off her pretty face? He clenched his fists, willing himself to stay away from her this time. She was the last thing he needed in his life.

"You read my column?" Lily asked, her smile widening to a full-fledged grin. "If you need some advice, all you have to do is ask. I'm here for you, Brax."

He scowled. "I wasn't reading your column for advice. I wanted to be prepared for the next crazy scheme you put into someone's head."

"And yet you weren't at all prepared for Cynthee," she teased with a wink.

Sage laughed, and when Braxton glared at her, she only laughed harder. "I'm sorry. But who could have predicted that someone would actually follow Lily's advice? Especially in broad daylight, right here in downtown Befana Bay?"

"How was I supposed to prepare for that?" Braxton asked, exasperated. Then he shook his head, wondering why he was so worked up. He knew that Lily's column was satire and that she wasn't to blame for some random woman's poor decision-making. Why was he taking his frustration out on her?

He knew why. It was because he couldn't stop thinking

about her. All that silky blond hair and her quick wit. Everything about her just did it for him. He really needed to figure out how to get her off his mind. Instead, he was standing on the street, griping at her because he'd had to deal with a flasher who otherwise could have just asked him out. He'd have said no, of course. Braxton didn't date. Not these days. It was far too problematic. It was why he had to stay away from Lily... no matter how much he wanted her.

"For the love of goddesses everywhere!" Lily threw her hands up. "My column is satire. You do understand what that means, don't you? The disclaimer is right there under my byline."

"I'm not an idiot," Braxton mumbled but realized he wasn't doing a good job of proving it.

Lily gave him a skeptical look but said nothing as she took her sister's arm and started leading her up the street.

Yeah, she might have had a point.

"Smooth, boss," Dante, his best friend and newly hired assistant manager, said from the open front door. He was standing against the doorjamb, his arms crossed over his chest, with an amused expression on his face. "You need some tips on how to talk to women? If so, let me know. I'll give you the friends-and-family discount."

"Funny," Braxton said dryly. "I thought you were working on inventory?"

"I was, but it looks like I finished just in time to see the show."

"You're not helping." Braxton brushed past Dante and strode back into the store, ready to forget the afternoon ever happened. "Let's just get back to work."

"Sure, boss," Dante called after him and added, "But that offer still stands, you know, if you need some help in the woman department!"

Braxton flipped the man off, praying for the day he could give him hell over someone he was dating. Unfortunately, the man was on a dry streak after a broken engagement six months earlier.

Not that I'm dating Lily, he reminded himself.

Once they were both back in the shop with Braxton behind the counter and Dante reorganizing a display of hiking trail books, Dante looked over at him and asked, "Why didn't you just ask her out?"

"Who? Cynthee?" Braxton asked, horrified. He'd liked the woman the few times he'd chatted with her in the store, but he'd never seen her that way. And after the debacle outside, he knew that even if he was in a position to date, he couldn't see them coming back from that mess.

"No, dude, I mean Lily. It's obvious you're into her, and she's perfect for you."

Braxton shook his head. "That's not going to happen."

"Why not?"

"It's complicated."

Dante gave him a disbelieving look. "It's actually pretty straightforward. You just call her up and ask her to dinner."

If Dante was anyone else, Braxton would shut him down and tell him to mind his own business. But they'd been friends since high school, well before they'd started working together just a few weeks ago. After Dante's broken engagement, he'd tried to stick it out back in Salem but found himself needing a change of scenery, and when

Braxton offered him a job, he'd jumped at it. They'd both been happy to be near each other again after years of distance. And if there was one person he could confide in, it was Dante. Still, Braxton held back, not ready to divulge his reasons for keeping Lily at arm's length. "There are… extenuating circumstances. It's just not a good idea."

"Extenuating circumstances?" Dante asked with an incredulous laugh. "What does that mean? Did you get married while I was living Back East these past few years and have a wife hidden somewhere or something?"

Braxton let out his own bark of laughter. "I wish it was that simple."

Dante frowned at him, his expression suddenly serious as he peered at Braxton. "Dude, you're acting stranger than usual. Are you going to tell me what's going on with you?"

"Now is not the time," Braxton said as the bell chimed above the door. He'd tell Dante eventually. When he didn't feel like he was going to throw up from just thinking about it.

"Braxton! There you are." Bethany Befana floated into the sporting goods store, looking like she'd just stepped out of a coven meeting. She was wearing a long, flowing, black-lace dress, red lace-up boots, and a collection of crystals around her neck. She was a powerful witch who lived in the large house at the end of Witch Tower Road and seemed to be the witch who watched over everything in Befana Bay.

"I didn't realize I was lost," Braxton said, happy for the distraction from his conversation with Dante. "What can I do for you today?"

"As you know, the midsummer celebration is coming

up." She placed a light hand on his bicep. "And I was hoping you could help me with a few of the details."

"Sure," he said automatically, always happy to help with any of the town events. He'd felt like an outsider most of his life, and it wasn't until he'd moved to Befana Bay that he'd felt like part of a community. He knew that was a direct result of being willing to chip in whenever needed. "Anything you need."

"Excellent. I was hoping you'd say that." She gave him a warm smile, but then it quickly faded as she studied him.

"What is it?" he asked automatically.

"When's the last time you had your energy cleared? It's feeling pretty heavy."

He glanced away. "Not too long ago. Nothing seems to last long."

She narrowed her eyes at him. "I bet I have just the thing. Are you free tomorrow afternoon? We'll do that cleansing and then talk about the midsummer celebration."

Braxton knew her cleansing wouldn't work. The only one who could clear his dark energy was his mother, and the gods knew that wasn't going to happen. Still, he nodded, knowing he wasn't going to be able to talk her out of trying. "I'll be there. Just let me know the time."

"Four o'clock for afternoon tea. Come hungry." She winked at him and then slipped out of the store.

"Afternoon tea?" Dante asked with a quirked eyebrow. "As in crustless sandwiches and fruity herbal tea?"

"I'm not much of a fan of the tea, but Bethany's scones are worth the price of admission," Braxton said with a chuckle.

"If you say so." Dante shook his head and went back to work reorganizing the displays.

Braxton disappeared into the back of the store to his office, relieved to have avoided another conversation about his nonexistent dating life.

CHAPTER 3

Dear Endora,

I've been best friends with a guy since college. We engage in lots of flirty, casual touching and cuddling, and all our friends are convinced we're in love with each other. Honestly, they are right when it comes to me. He's the love of my life, but I can't seem to get him to see me as anything other than a friend. What should I do to get his attention?

Signed, Destined to always be the bestie

Dear Bestie,

Clearly this calls for drastic measures. Make a "date" for drinks with your bestie at the local pub. Pull out all the stops. Get your hair done. Wax everything. Wear your sexiest outfit and your six-inch F^%$ me heels. When you show up, have one drink with him and then kiss him as if you're going to drag him into the coat closet. Then just leave him there, gaping after you. He'll be showing up at your door in twenty minutes.

Alternatively, you could do the adult thing and just talk to him about your feelings. Your choice.

Endora

Lily hit Send to fire off her latest column to her editor and then closed her laptop. She knew she should be working on her book, but it was a gorgeous day in the Pacific Northwest, and she wanted to be outside enjoying her flower garden. There were weeds to pull and deadheading to do. And then she'd cut some blooms for a bouquet for her dining room table.

After grabbing her gardening gloves and shears from her closet, she walked out onto the front porch and was just about to get started when her phone buzzed. Her grandmother's name flashed across the screen, making her smile.

Bethany Befana was just about her favorite person in the world. She loved everything about the eccentric witch. "Hello, Gran. You just caught me before I got to work in the gardens."

"Oh dear," she said, sounding apologetic. "I'm sorry to interrupt. I know how much you enjoy communing with the earth."

Don't most witches? Lily thought, but she just said, "It's no problem. What's up?"

"Well, I was hoping you could come by this afternoon. I have a favor to ask."

Lily glanced at her watch. It was just before four. She supposed her gardens could wait an hour or two. "Sure. You want me to come now?"

"That would be wonderful. I have tea ready."

Lily grinned. Of course she did. Her grandmother was the master of buttering people up when she wanted something. "All right. Let me clean up and I'll be over in about twenty minutes."

"Thank you, dear. I can't wait to see you."

Lily put her gardening stuff away and went back inside to tidy her hair and put on clean clothes. Being a writer meant she was rarely ready to go anywhere at a moment's notice. Not when she was used to working in T-shirts and yoga pants. Since her grandmother was serving tea, she decided to wear a casual maxi dress and sandals. Then she put her hair up into an easy twist. After checking herself in the mirror, she decided she didn't look half bad for her fifteen-minute makeover.

With a sweater in hand, Lily walked out of her small two-bedroom cottage and headed two blocks over to her grandmother's large Victorian. The gorgeous place never failed to evoke warm memories. This was her home. Where she grew up. Where she'd felt safe after she and her sisters had lost both their parents as children. Lily barely remembered her father. He'd passed when she was just an infant. Her mother had been taken when Lily was in the fourth grade. It had been traumatic, but Bethany had stepped right in and had proven to be Lily's safe place ever since.

Lily knocked once before striding into the foyer. "I made it," she called as she headed toward the dining room, where she knew her grandmother would be.

"Oh good. You're just in time," Bethany called back.

"For what?" Lily turned the corner into the dining room

and came to an abrupt stop when she spotted Braxton Kirkwood sitting to the right of her grandmother.

He stood abruptly, hitting the table and making the tea tray sway. Water sloshed from the full glasses, leaving wet marks on the pale pink tablecloth. "Oh, no. I'm so sorry, Bethany," he said, grabbing the table to settle it.

"It's fine, dear. It's only water." She rose from her seat and nearly floated over to Lily. Cupping her granddaughter's cheeks, Bethany kissed her forehead and said, "Thanks for coming at the last minute."

"Sure, Grandmother. You know I'd do anything for you." The statement was true, but as she eyed Braxton, she wondered what exactly Bethany was up to. She loved her grandmother with all her heart, but she didn't always love the way Bethany meddled in her granddaughters' lives. If this was a setup, she was going to be annoyed. Lily was done thinking about the man who was too attractive for her own good.

"Braxton here needs an energy cleanse," Bethany said, waving a hand in his direction. "I could use your help with the cleansing spell."

"Oh, no, I'm sure Lily doesn't—" Braxton started.

"Of course. Happy to help," Lily said, cutting him off as she eyed him. Her grandmother had always been good at reading auras and energy. It wasn't one of Lily's gifts, but that didn't mean she couldn't help with a cleansing spell.

"We don't need to do this right now," Braxton said, sounding as if he'd rather be handling toxic waste than dealing with an energy cleansing.

"Don't be silly," Bethany said. "Lily's here now. This will

take no time at all. Come with me." She swept out of the dining room and into an adjoining sunroom.

Lily gave him a sympathetic smile. "She won't change her mind. Might as well just get it over with."

Braxton hesitated for a long moment and then finally followed Bethany into the room where her grandmother made her herbal creations.

Lily stood by the entrance with her arms crossed over her chest as her grandmother mixed a bowl of herbs at a wooden butcher block that was pushed up against the wall.

When Bethany was done, she carried the herbs and a candle into the middle of the room and waved both Braxton and Lily over. "Here, Braxton, you hold the candle. And Lily, you take the herbs."

Both of them did as Bethany said.

"Ready?" the older witch asked.

"No," Braxton said at the same time that Lily said, "Yes."

Lily chuckled. "Just relax, Braxton. It's painless."

"You hope," he grumbled.

Bethany chuckled. "She's right. It is." Then she raised her arms and started chanting her spell in Latin.

Braxton stood stock-still, looking like a deer in the headlights.

Lily wanted to reach out and hold his hand, show him some support. But that would interrupt the spell. Not everyone was super comfortable with spells, and it looked like Braxton was one of them.

"Now, Lily!" Bethany called.

Lily poured the herbs into her palm and then blew them toward Braxton. They immediately caught on the air and swirled around Braxton as Bethany finished her chant.

Bethany threw her hands up in the air at the same moment the flame flickered to life on the candle, and the swirl of herbs intensified.

Then suddenly, the herbs disappeared and the candle went out.

Silence filled the sunroom as the light shown over Braxton in an ethereal glow.

Braxton blinked and then let out a small laugh. "That was... incredible."

Bethany smiled. "See, I told you it was painless. Let's go in and have our tea."

As Bethany moved into the next room, Lily took the candle from him and placed it on the workstation. She eyed him, "Feeling better?"

He nodded. "Lighter than I have in ages."

"Good." She slipped her arm through his and led him back into the dining room, pleased that they were able to help him.

Bethany was standing at her place at the head of the table. "Take a seat. We have much to discuss."

"I bet we do," Lily muttered as she sat to the right of her grandmother, realizing that her summons hadn't just been about clearing Braxton's energy.

Braxton gave her a curious stare and then turned his attention back to Bethany, and Lily guessed that he'd been just as surprised by her presence this afternoon as she was about his.

"So, Gran," Lily said in an overly sweet tone as her

grandmother poured the tea. "What exactly do you have to discuss with both me and Braxton?"

"I'm glad you asked," she said with a pleasant smile as if she didn't know that Lily was annoyed. "As you know, the midsummer celebration is coming up in a few weeks."

"Yes," Lily said, eyeballing her. "Isn't Cassandra in charge of that?" Cassandra was one of Bethany's friends and a longtime coven member.

"She was until she completely dropped the ball," Bethany said with a sniff. "I knew she was always planning things right up until the last minute, but I didn't realize what a terrible procrastinator she actually is until just yesterday when she dropped it all in my lap. It turns out she hadn't gotten anything done and then accepted a last-minute invitation to Transylvania from an online lover. She left early this morning, and I'm going to need some help if this year's celebration is still going to happen."

"And we're it?" Lily asked, glancing at Braxton.

"Yes!" she said with a gleam in her eye. "You're just so organized, Lily. If anyone can pull this off, it's you. And Braxton has all the resources for the games. I figured, together you would be the perfect pair."

Perfect pair. Lily knew her grandmother didn't just mean celebration planning. She'd heard all about the kiss that had happened at the Witches Ball. And if she had to guess, one of her sisters had likely informed her about the one that happened after August's gallery opening, too. This wasn't just an SOS for help on a town event; this was a setup. Lily knew it down to her bones. When it came to love matches for her granddaughters, Bethany just couldn't leave well enough alone.

Braxton cleared his throat. "What all are you looking for?"

A cat-that-ate-the-canary grin took over Bethany's features, and Lily couldn't help but roll her eyes. Her grandmother was a piece of work. "I knew I could count on you, dear. I'll need you to organize the games portion of the celebration. There's the individual paddleboard, enchanted bike, and broom races, plus the triathlon of all three. Oh, and the team stylized synchronized broom and enchanted bike competitions."

"Don't forget the magical corn hole and crochet," Lily said, unable to stop herself, even though she wanted to strangle her grandmother. She couldn't help it. The midsummer celebration was one of her favorite events of the year.

"That's right," Bethany said with a nod. "Lily and her sisters have their crochet title to defend. You've never seen a more competitive team."

Lily chuckled. It was true. The four of them were ruthless when it came to magical crochet. They were on a five-year winning streak.

"I look forward to the spectacle," Braxton said.

"Then there are the food vendors, the arts and crafts vendors, and I want to have a ball for another fundraiser."

Lily swallowed a groan and forced herself not to look at Braxton. She didn't want to recall what happened the last time they were both at a ball. "Fundraise for what?" she asked.

"I want to raise money for the youth witch summer program that has been struggling ever since poor Mr. Frankenlily got conned into purchasing those 'elusive' toadstools that were said to turn stones into gold."

"I take it they didn't work?" Braxton asked.

"Nope." Bethany passed each of them a scone and then gestured to the clotted cream and the lemon curd that was on the table as she continued. "The toadstools were actually just psychedelic mushrooms the grifter used to scam old hippy witches. If we don't do something, the summer program is going to go broke, and the youngsters of this town will be seriously lacking on their education in basic spells and magical tradition. Now that the schools think teaching witchcraft isn't essential, most are cutting their entire programs. We need to do something to help fill in the gaps. Would you mind terribly putting that together while organizing the celebration? It would mean the world to me."

"Absolutely. I'd be happy to help," Braxton said immediately.

Lily stared at him, wishing intentions alone could curse someone. Did he have any idea how much work all of that was going to be? And if he pawned it all off on her, they were going to have some serious words. "Grandmother," Lily said slowly. "That is a tough order when the celebration is in just two weeks."

"I know, dear, but I have my hands full with the new tarot school as well as the art showcase. If this had happened at any other time, I'd be available to help organize it all, but right now, my hands are tied."

Lily very much doubted her time was that limited, but

what was she going to do, say no? Absolutely not. She'd just enlist as many of her sisters as she could to help. "Fine, but you owe me."

Bethany patted her hand. "Consider me indebted." She turned to Braxton, who'd just shoved half of a scone into his mouth. "Tell me all about the flasher outside your store yesterday. I heard it was quite the show."

Braxton sputtered, spewing crumbs out onto the pristine table. His cheeks flushed deep red as he hurried to clean up his mess. After he swallowed, he glanced up and said, "Sorry about that. You caught me a little off guard."

Bethany's eyes gleamed as she said, "It seems like that's happening to you a lot lately."

After they finished their tea and Braxton left, Lily helped her grandmother clear the table. Once they were in the kitchen, Lily cornered her by the sink. "I know what you're doing. You know that, right?"

"What am I doing?" Bethany placed a hand on her chest and gave Lily an innocent look. "If you mean that I'm trying to make sure one of the town's most popular events doesn't get canceled due to Cassandra's poor planning, then yes. You're a hundred percent right. That's what I'm doing."

"No, I mean the bit about you pairing me up with Braxton. Just because we kissed that one time doesn't mean it's a good idea for us to date. Your meddling won't change that."

Bethany let out a huff of surprise. "Meddling? That's quite an accusation."

"A true one. But don't get your hopes up. Braxton isn't my type."

"If you say so, honey," Bethany said as she turned to the sink and started loading dishes into the dishwasher.

"I do," Lily said.

"Sure." Bethany shrugged. "I heard you. You could be right, but I guess we'll just have to wait and see."

"You're going to be waiting a long time," Lily called as she made her way toward the front door.

"I'm not in a hurry," her grandmother proclaimed in a singsong voice.

Lily scowled and muttered, "Meddlesome old crow."

"I heard that!" Bethany called.

"I wasn't trying to be quiet!" Lily called back, but she was grinning to herself as she slipped out of the old house. Even though she was irritated that her grandmother was interfering in her nonexistent love life, she couldn't stay mad at her. How could she? Lily knew her grandmother just wanted her to be happy. It was all she'd ever wanted for her granddaughters. And Lily knew that no matter what, if she needed *anything*, Bethany Befana would be there for her.

It was why she vowed to make the midsummer celebration one of the best they'd ever had. Her grandmother had asked for help, and Lily didn't plan to let her down.

CHAPTER 4

BRAXTON PLACED a vase full of hydrangeas from his garden in the middle of his table and wondered if it was too much. He'd set the table and taken one look at the pillar candle in the middle and decided that wouldn't do at all. This wasn't a romantic date. This was a planning session.

The flowers were a mistake, too. It definitely looked like he was trying too hard. He picked them up and placed them on the butcherblock sideboard.

That was better.

"Seriously, man, I think you've lost your marbles," Dante said.

Braxton looked up at his friend and then cupped the back of his neck with one hand, massaging the tense muscles. "No kidding."

Dante glanced around at the homemade manicotti and tossed salad and raised both eyebrows. "Are you sure this isn't a date?"

"It's definitely not a date," Braxton insisted. "I already told you; we're planning—"

"The midsummer celebration. Yeah. I heard you the first time. I guess if it were me, I'd have just ordered pizza and gotten a six pack instead of spending all afternoon cooking pasta and uncorking that fancy wine. What is it again?"

"Don't worry about it." Braxton didn't appreciate his friend needling him. So what if he liked pasta and wine? Who didn't?

"It's Italian," Dante said with a laugh as he peered at the bottle. "This is definitely a date."

"Get out. Lily will be here any minute, and we have work to do," Braxton grumbled.

"Text me the code word if you need me to stay away tonight."

"I'm not going to need you to stay away," Braxton said. "And what code word?"

Dante threw his head back and cackled. "See, you need it just in case."

"I don't need it," Braxton insisted.

"If you say so." Dante moved toward the front door. "I'm headed to the pub. If things heat up around here, just remember the code word is Peter."

"I'm not gonna text you!" Braxton called out over Dante's laughter.

The door slammed closed, and Braxton looked at his table. "Dammit, it does look like a date."

"It looks and smells wonderful," a familiar voice said from behind him.

Braxton spun to find Lily standing in his dining room,

holding a notebook and looking lovelier than ever. Her long blond hair was down and cascading in waves over her shoulders, and instead of a dress like she'd worn the day before at her grandmother's, she had on formfitting blue plaid pants and a silky white blouse that hugged all the right curves. "Uh, hi. I didn't realize you were already here."

"Dante let me in. I hope that's all right."

"Of course it is," he said automatically and stuffed his hands in his pockets.

A few seconds of silence ticked by until Lily chuckled. "So, looks like you made dinner?"

"I should have ordered pizza." Braxton grabbed the wine bottle and poured two glasses.

"I prefer this," Lily said, waving at the pan of manicotti. "It smells amazing."

"I hope it lives up. Take a seat." He pulled her chair out for her and immediately regretted it. *Not a date. Not a date. Not a date*, he reminded himself. Why was he acting like a nervous sixteen-year-old?

This was a work meeting. Nothing more.

"How are you feeling today?" Lily asked.

"Fine. Why?"

"Just curious if the energy cleansing my grandmother did yesterday made any difference."

"Ah, yes, actually," he said, feeling himself relax as he smiled at her. The cleansing had made him feel lighter, and he had more energy than he'd had in ages. "Your grandmother was very kind doing that for me."

"She lives for that kind of thing," Lily said.

"Please, thank her again for me," Braxton said as he

plated both of their dinners and then took a seat. With his wine glass in hand, he said, "So, which tasks are you interested in taking?"

Lily looked up from her plate of manicotti and blinked at him. "Sorry?"

"With our tight time constraints, I figured the best thing to do was to divide and conquer. I thought—"

"Whoa. Hold on." Lily put her fork down and leaned forward. "Have you *met* my grandmother?"

"What are you getting at, Lily?" Braxton asked, keeping his gaze on hers.

She let out a huff of laughter. "Bethany Befana is the most meticulous person either of us have ever met. And as much as I'd like to take half the list and run with it, we can't do that. My grandmother is a very particular woman, and if everything isn't perfect, I will never hear the end of it. Besides, she asked us to work together, and if she finds out we didn't… Well, you probably don't want to live through that judgment. Trust me. We do this together or not at all."

So his instincts were right. She didn't necessarily want to be working with him and had only agreed to appease her grandmother. Well, what did he expect? He hadn't exactly been jumping at the chance to spend the next two weeks with her either, had he? Hadn't he been the one who'd tried to split up the list? But deep down, he knew he'd only done that because being around her was damn near torture. All he wanted to do was reach out and tuck a lock of her hair behind her ear. But instead, he looked down at his dinner and nodded. "Yeah, I can see that. So, where do we start?"

"Organizing the competitions so we can get signups ready to post," she said, pulling out a notebook.

"Right." He launched into his vision for each of the races and the triathlon.

Lily frantically took notes, nodding along and adding a few suggestions here and there. But overall, they seemed to be on the same page. Then they moved onto the magical corn hole and the crochet competitions.

Once they had those mapped out and scheduled, they finished their dinner and each had another glass of wine. Braxton cleared the dishes and then asked, "Okay, what next? Should we tackle the food vendors?"

"Yes, but—wait! I just had another idea." She grinned up at him. "What about a floral arranging competition and a Best in Show blue ribbon for the craft corner? People can donate a few bucks to enter, and someone will walk away with bragging rights."

"Both of those sound like great ideas." Braxton moved over closer to Lily and started drawing a map on one of her notebook pages, wanting to make sure they were going to have room on the waterfront for all the activities.

"I like that setup," Lily said, leaning over his shoulder. Then she glanced up at him. "Your map is fantastic. Do you ever draw or paint for fun?"

"I used to," he admitted and felt a surge of pride from her praise. He hadn't shared his drawings with hardly anyone. They were just too personal. However, he liked that Lily knew something about him that most people didn't.

"Used to? Why'd you stop?" she asked, her expression full of curiosity.

"Life, I guess." He shrugged. "There never seems to be enough time." It was a lie, but he wasn't going to go into the reasons why he never picked up a paintbrush or sketchbook anymore.

"It happens. But if you enjoy it, you really should set aside some time just for yourself. You clearly don't work *all* the time. You're here with me, aren't you?"

She had him there. "Yeah. You're probably right. Maybe I'll think about it."

"Maybe." Her lips twitched with amusement as she shook her head. "Sounds exactly like what one says when they have zero plans to do something."

He laughed. "You're not wrong."

Lily nudged him with her shoulder and then flipped her notebook to a new page. "We need to recruit some food vendors. Any ideas?"

They discussed various food trucks to invite, but after calling a few, they learned there was another event being held south of Befana Bay that same week, and only one vendor had an extra truck available for the midsummer celebration.

"We need to brainstorm some ideas, or we're going to have to set up a grill and serve hotdogs," Lily said.

"It'd have to be more than one grill," Braxton added with a frown. "And we'd need a lot of grill handlers to volunteer. There have to be other food trucks around here somewhere."

"Over on the island?" Lily asked.

"Crystal Point Island?" Braxton asked, wondering why they'd have a bunch of food trucks. It was a small island, mostly made up of summer homes and not much in the way of tourism shops.

"No. Westerly. They have plenty of summer festivals, but none are on the island calendar during our event. See?" She turned her computer so that he could see what she was looking at. "They don't have anything scheduled until July 4th. If we're lucky, we might find everything we need over there."

Braxton nodded. "That could work. Are you free tomorrow to head to the island and see if we can get some samples?" While there weren't any events happening, the island's food trucks would likely still be parked somewhere, open for business.

"I can make time." Lily pulled up the ferry schedule. The island was about twenty-five miles from Befana Bay, but the only way to get there was by ferry. "It leaves every hour on the hour. So which one do you want to take? The ten or eleven o'clock?"

He huffed. "I was thinking the eight. If we go later, we'll waste half the day away, and I do still need to tend to my store at some point."

She gave him a strange look. "You think the food trucks are going to be open at 9:00 a.m.? Have you ever eaten at one?"

"Oh, right." Braxton felt like an idiot. What was he thinking? Obviously, most of them wouldn't open until lunch. "Then I'll go into work first thing and meet you for the ferry at ten. Sound good?"

"Sounds perfect." Lily shut her notebook and pushed her chair back. "I think that's enough planning for tonight. We can finish the craft fair stuff while we're on the ferry tomorrow."

Disappointed she was leaving, Braxton stood and walked her to the door.

"It was a good night, Brax," she said, using his nickname for the first time since she'd walked in. "You're easier to work with than I thought you might be."

"I'm not sure if I should be flattered or offended," he said with a huff of laughter.

"Flattered, definitely," she said as she patted his chest just over his heart. Then she pressed up on her toes and kissed him on the cheek. "And there wasn't even one inappropriate stripper."

"Something to save for next time."

Lily laughed, and it made Braxton want to wrap her in his arms and ask her to stay. Instead, he took a step back and said, "See you in the morning, Lily."

She paused and then cleared her throat before she said, "Thank you for dinner. It was lovely."

Braxton nodded, unsure of what to say, but it didn't matter because in the next moment, she disappeared out his front door and hurried down the street toward her small cottage that sat just a few houses from the water's edge. He stood at his window, watching her until she was safely inside her house.

He didn't move for a long moment, happy to bask in the glow of a wonderful evening with a woman he liked entirely too much. It wasn't until he heard his phone buzz that he retreated. And since it was well past ten in the evening, he figured it was either Dante checking to see if it was clear for him to return, or Lily, who might have thought of something else for the celebration.

Braxton strode over to the table, grabbed his phone, and scowled.

It was neither Dante nor Lily.

It was his mother.

He debated before answering it. There wasn't anything stopping him from ignoring her call. But if he did, he knew she'd just blow up his phone until he finally answered.

It probably would have been easier to just take the call and get it over with, but he just couldn't. Not after the pleasant night he'd had with Lily. He was in far too good a mood to deal with his mother. That would have to wait for another day.

After the phone rang nonstop for nearly ten minutes, the noise finally stopped until his voice mail notification chimed.

He stared at the phone like it was a rattlesnake that would bite him if he touched it. But he finally just sucked it up and listened.

"Baby, it's your mother. Well, obviously. I'm calling from my number, so you know that. I was really hoping we could chat and maybe finally put our differences behind us. I know you're angry, but surely enough time has lapsed that we can finally reconnect and put everything that happened behind us. You know, start being a family again." She rattled off her number as if he didn't already have it and then said, "Call me, baby. Anytime."

Braxton didn't even consider calling her. He immediately deleted the message and then fumed as he paced his kitchen. She had some nerve. How dare she call and act like everything was just fine? As if he'd been a toddler who'd needed to get a tantrum out of his system.

He'd already told her in no uncertain terms that he didn't want to have anything to do with her while she was selling potions and curses on the black market.

But the real nail in the coffin was when she'd sold one of her curses to his crazy ex, knowing she was going to use it on him. And that was how Braxton Kirkwood's love life had ended up cursed.

His own mother didn't have even one shred of decency in her entire body, and now her son would pay for it for the rest of his life.

"Call her?" He let out a humorless laugh and shook his head. "Hell no."

CHAPTER 5

Lily smiled to herself as she spotted Braxton pacing in front of the ferry entrance. His brow was furrowed, and there was an air of nervousness surrounding him. It was the same energy she'd encountered the day before when she'd met him at his house for dinner. She wasn't sure why, but it was clear that she had gotten under his skin and was frustrating him in the best possible way.

The best part of the day would be finding out just how long it took for him to shed his anxiety and finally start to relax. In the meantime, she'd enjoy poking the bear until he came out of his shell.

"Good morning, sunshine," she said cheerfully when she was close.

Braxton jerked his head up, looking startled to see her.

"You didn't forget that I was joining you on this adventure, did you?" she asked, her lips quirking into a teasing smile.

"What? No, I was just thinking about a phone call I got last night." He shoved his hands into his pockets and shook his head. "I was sort of lost in thought."

She raised both eyebrows. "Everything okay?"

"Yeah, of course. Just parent stuff. I'm sure you know how it is," he said absently as he turned his attention to the ticket booth.

She didn't. Not really. Her parents had both died when she was young, leaving her with no real frame of reference for adult parent relationships. There was her grandmother of course, but Lily's relationship with her had always seemed so different than that of her friends and their parents, so she didn't bother answering. Instead, she pulled out a few bills and put them on the ticket counter.

Braxton snatched the money up and shoved it back at her. "I've got this."

"You don't need to pay for me, Braxton," Lily said, refusing to take the money back.

"Why do you always have to be so stubborn?" he asked as he tucked the money into the front pocket of her handbag.

"I'm not stubborn. Just independent," she said as she rolled her eyes. "Fine. You get the ferry. I'll get lunch."

Braxton handed her one of the tickets as they made their way onto the ramp. "That's not exactly a fair exchange. Lunch is going to be more than the four dollars I just plunked down for walk-on passage."

"That's what you get for not accepting my money," Lily said with a grin, enjoying the exchange. Normally she wouldn't make a big deal out of letting someone pay for her. She figured when it came to friends and family paying for events, they would just take turns and it all came out in the wash in the end. But poking Braxton about it was just too much fun.

He groaned and followed her onto the ferry. They made their way up the stairs to the enclosed seating area and took a spot at a table by a window.

Lily immediately pulled out her notebook and got down to business. She pointed to the open pages. "I did a layout for the craft fair last night. If we position the booths like this, I think we can accommodate everyone who has already shown interest." Her grandmother had given her a list of craftspeople who'd already applied, despite Cassandra's poor organizational skills. It seemed activating the online interest form was the *one* thing she'd actually done a few months ago.

Braxton studied her drawing, made a couple of suggestions, and then nodded. "That looks great. If everything goes this smoothly, we'll have this done in no time."

"Oh no. Don't jinx us like that," Lily said with a laugh and then quickly sobered when he frowned. "What?"

"Nothing." He shook his head and then pulled out a small notebook of his own. "I wrote down a list of the food truck vendors and put them in two lists. One is in order by distance from the ferry, and the other prioritizes the ones that I thought looked most interesting." He pushed the notebook toward Lily. "Take a look."

She glanced down at his meticulous handwriting and shook her head in disbelief. "You seriously spent your evening doing this last night?"

"Yeah. Why? Is that strange or something?" he asked, looking confused.

"No, not at all." She laughed and flipped her own notebook to the pages where she'd done something similar. "I also put them in order according to distance from the ferry. But my second list is ranked by which has the highest online reviews."

They both laughed and then got down to business comparing the lists.

"Looks like we're mostly on the same page," Braxton said.

"Looks like it." Lily looked up at him with a warm feeling in her chest. It had been forever since she'd felt this comfortable with a man. She was surprised to find that she was actually looking forward to spending the day with him. But then the image of him bolting after he'd kissed her flashed through her mind, and she had to suppress a scowl.

What was it with her being attracted to emotionally unavailable men? She'd spent much of her college days in and out of a relationship with a man who'd run hot and cold. And after he'd promised her the world and then ghosted her the day they were supposed to move in together, she'd vowed to never put herself through that again. Never. It didn't matter that Braxton Kirkwood looked and kissed like a god. Or that every time she spent any time with him it felt like coming home. She would not set herself up for disappointment again.

Not this time. This time she'd be smart.

"Lily, look," Braxton said, placing his hand over hers.

A tingle ran up her arm, causing gooseflesh to pop out

over her bare skin. She quickly pulled her hand away and said, "Huh?"

His gaze was locked on her hand that she'd tucked into the arm of her sweatshirt. With a small frown he looked up at her face, and whatever he saw in her expression made him glance away again. He pointed out the window. "Orcas."

Lily turned and spotted a familiar orca breeching the surface. The majestic orca Tokia turned midair, showing the white underside of her body as she splashed into the water. And then a smaller orca, Tokia's baby, Kyia, followed suit, making everyone on the ferry cheer. Lily's eyes were damp when she turned back to Braxton and breathed, "Oh gosh, she's doing wonderfully, isn't she?"

"She is." They smiled softly at each other.

In recent years, due to pollution and overfishing of the Salish sea, it had become harder and harder for the orca populations to reproduce. The success rate of newborn orcas had been dwindling, and much to the horror of the witches of Befana Bay, the pod had lost two babies in the last few years. But Kyia had made it past three months, which was a critical milestone, and she appeared to be thriving. She was the pride of Befana Bay.

Lily finally pulled her gaze away from Braxton, realizing that the ferry had stopped while the orcas put on a show for them. More members of the pod breeched the water, flipping their tails and fins as they swam around baby Kyia, clearly celebrating the life of the baby orca.

A single tear ran down Lily's cheek as she watched the orcas finally head north away from the ferry. Braxton silently handed her a tissue, making her chuckle softly.

"Sorry. I just get so emotional when the orcas are around. They are such special creatures."

"No need to apologize," he said. "They are magical."

In more ways than one. The witches of Befana Bay had a special connection to the orcas. In fact, they often visited the witches when they gathered at sunrise on their paddleboards in the bay. The peaceful power they possessed was awe-inspiring.

Lily and Braxton both seemed to be lost in their own thoughts as the ferry finally docked at Westerly Island. They were silent as they made their way into the quaint downtown that was filled with small galleries, a couple of farm-to-table restaurants, a coffee shop, an ice creamery, a bookstore, and a pretty Victorian inn that overlooked the Puget Sound.

"I've always wondered what it would be like to live on the island," Lily finally said. "I could never leave Befana Bay, but it just seems like life moves at a slower pace here. Almost like it's removed from the modern world in a way."

Braxton snorted. "You think Befana Bay isn't removed from the modern world? There's magic everywhere you look."

Lily had to laugh. He had a point. The enchanted town definitely marched to the beat of its own drum. "You've got a point. I suppose there's just a romance to the island because the only way to get to it is the ferry."

"I can see that," Braxton said, his voice suddenly gruff.

Lily glanced up at him, but he'd turned away and was leading her toward their first food truck.

"Crab cakes eighteen ways," Braxton read from the sign of Grab You by the Crab.

"I *love* crab," Lily said as she walked up to the window and ordered three different kinds.

"I can see that." Braxton ordered the crab cake cheese melt, and after a short wait, they took their food to a picnic table.

Lily dug into her fried green tomato crab cake and moaned her pleasure with the first bite.

Braxton cleared his throat and shifted on his seat as he glanced away, his cheeks flushing red.

Lily felt heat rush to her own cheeks as she realized what she must have sounded like and made a mental note to keep her sounds to herself for the rest of the day. "This place is a must-book," she said, putting her fork down. "I'm going to go see if the owner is here and lock them down if at all possible."

Braxton nodded, and Lily quickly hurried back over to the truck.

Five minutes later, she returned with a triumphant grin on her face. "They're in! One down, about ten to go."

"Perfect. I hope you've been in training for this, because after eating all that, I don't know how we're going to sample nine more trucks."

She glanced at her paper bowls of half-eaten food and nodded. "Yeah. Better pace ourselves.

After three more trucks and three more bookings, Lily rubbed her stomach and let out a groan. "I'm never going to make it. I've lost all self-control when it comes to tasting all this food. You're going to have to try the rest of the trucks and let me know which we're going to book."

Braxton laughed. "You did see me devour that entire sushi roll, right? If I eat one more thing, I'm going to explode."

"Oh man. We're hopeless." Lily gave him a pathetic look that only made him laugh harder.

When he finally came up for air, he said, "Okay, let's take a bit of a break. There's a trail that leads to a crystal-clear lake in the middle of the island. How about we walk off a little bit of this food before we go in for the next round?"

"As long as I don't have to stick anything in my mouth for the next two hours," she agreed.

Braxton eyed her before his lips twitched into a sexy half-smile.

"Get your mind out of the gutter, Brax. You know what I meant," she said, swatting his arm playfully. "Now, which way is this trail?"

Without comment, Braxton led the short distance to the trailhead that led from the main road and quickly disappeared into the trees.

CHAPTER 6

SMALL TWIGS and brush snapped under Braxton's shoes as he led Lily along the Westerly Lake Trail. They'd been silent for a few minutes as they followed the well-worn path. Now that they'd taken a break from the food tasting, they seemed to have run out of things to say.

Or at least Lily had. Braxton had plenty of words right on the tip of his tongue. Like how he was having a really good time and wanted to ask her if she kayaked. And would she be willing to meet him in the mornings at sunrise for a trip through the bay? Or if she'd like to join him on his day off to explore the hiking trails around Befana Bay. He wanted to ask how she felt about Thai food and if she'd traveled outside of Befana Bay much. And he wanted to know all about her writing, how she'd gotten started, and if she ever wrote anything other than her advice column.

But he didn't say any of that. Instead, he focused on

putting one foot in front of the other and told himself that he needed to keep things between them strictly professional. Nothing good could come from getting closer to the gorgeous, feisty blonde. It would only mean heartbreak for one or both of them.

"What are you thinking so hard about?" Lily asked him.

Braxton's foot caught on an exposed root, and he stumbled, nearly sending him sprawling onto the dirt path, but he managed to get his feet underneath himself just in time.

"Whoa!" Lily reached out and caught his arm with both her hands, helping to steady him.

The entire left side of his body tingled from her touch, and he stood there staring at her hands for a moment, saying nothing.

Lily squeezed his arm gently and then frowned when she let go.

Braxton, realizing he was making things awkward, cleared his throat. "Thanks." And then he pasted on a smile as he lied through an explanation for his clumsiness. "That's what I get for thinking about work instead of just enjoying the great outdoors."

"It happens to the best of us," she said, giving him a small smile as she nodded toward the path in front of them. "We're almost to the lake."

As Lily took off in front of him, Braxton followed, trying to shake off the feeling that if he just stood by and let Lily Easton go, he'd be making the biggest mistake of his life. But how could he not? If he followed his heart and started something with her, misery was sure to follow.

Anger started to creep in around the edges, and all the glorious lightness that he'd felt ever since Bethany Befana had done that cleanse started to fade away. He wanted to rage at his ex, his mother, and the universe. Instead, he sucked in a deep breath and slowly let it out, doing his best to focus on the clean scent of the forest and the crisp cool air of the Pacific Northwest.

"Oh, wow," Lily said as the trees parted, and the bluest lake Braxton had ever seen came into view. She walked over to the edge of the water and paused, taking it all in. "I always forget how lovely this lake is."

"You've been here before then." It was a statement, not a question.

"A few times," she said with a shrug. "My mom brought us here once when I was younger, and then later I came with a friend when we were in our hiking era."

"Hiking era?" he asked, interested. "You don't hike anymore?"

"Oh, I do," she said, her features softening. "But my friend moved Back East, and now I don't have anyone who enjoys it as much as I do. So I tend to stick to busier trails just for safety reasons. And without a hiking partner, I tend not to get out as much. So this is a nice detour for me. Thanks for suggesting it."

"I hike, too," he blurted and then wished he'd kept his big mouth closed. Hadn't he just decided that getting closer to her was a terrible idea?

"Really?" Her eyes gleamed. "After this midsummer celebration is over, we should get out and try some trails."

Then she reigned in her excitement and added, "If you're up for it."

"Yes," he said before he could stop himself. When it came to Lily Easton, he just couldn't seem to say no.

"Great. I'd love that." Lily hooked her arm through his, and together they walked along the edge of the glistening lake.

When they reached a dock at a public picnic area, they stopped and sat on the edge, peering into the crystal-clear water.

"It's amazing that this exists," Lily said quietly.

Braxton raised his eyebrows at her. "The dock?"

"No, this." She waved her hand at the lake. "I mean, obviously, the wonder of nature and all that, but more so that it mostly remains untouched. That us humans haven't ruined it. That we can walk here from town and find it mostly deserted. No trash lining the shore. No residences with cars and boats that have claimed ownership. It's almost like something out of a dream."

"It's really something," he agreed. They'd encountered a couple of people on the trail, but Lily was right. They'd barely seen anyone that afternoon. He supposed it was the cool and overcast weather that was keeping people away. That and the fact that it was a workday. He supposed on the weekend the trail would be hopping with people. Still, at the moment, their time at the lake felt a little magical, and Braxton was so content that he couldn't help himself when he whispered, "I think I'd be happy living in this moment forever."

A rustle from the nearby trees startled them, and they

both turned to see a large white wolf come to a stop at the end of their dock.

Braxton stiffened and turned slightly, shielding Lily in case the wolf attacked. But the creature didn't feel threatening. He just stood there, watching with interest. Magic seemed to crackle in the air, sparking all around them and brushing lightly against Braxton's skin. He peered past the wolf, searching for a witch that might be traveling with the animal. But he didn't see anyone.

Lily placed her hand over Braxton's, squeezing softly, and Braxton could have sworn that the wolf's eyes focused on their connection. Then the wolf looked right at Braxton, his eyes flashing from gold to bright blue just before he turned and disappeared back into the trees.

"Wow," Lily whispered softly.

Braxton nodded, knowing they'd just witnessed something incredibly rare. He looked down at their joined hands and, for once, didn't feel the urge to bolt.

His gaze met Lily's, and the attraction was there. That pull that had compelled him to kiss her twice before. He couldn't help it when he focused on her lips and remembered what it felt like to have her in his arms, to have her pressed up against him, tasting her. Wanting her.

Lily cleared her throat. "We should probably get back to town and finish our taste-testing mission before they close up for the day."

"Right." Braxton jerked his gaze away from her sweet lips and stood quickly. Holding a hand out to her, he helped her to her feet and then quickly shoved his hands into his pockets to keep from touching her again.

Lily gave him a searching look before quickly shaking her head. Then she headed off the dock and back onto the trail. "Let's get a move on. We still have a lot to do before we catch that last ferry."

Braxton jogged to catch up until he fell into step beside her. Neither said anything for a long moment before Brax finally broke the silence. "I didn't know there were wolves in this part of the state."

"I've heard there have been a few sightings," Lily said. "But none that were magical."

"You felt it, too?" Brax glanced at her and quickly looked away, afraid he'd start staring at her lips again.

"Sure did. I don't know what it means. Maybe he walks this life with a witch here on the island," Lily said. "I've heard about a witch in Keating Hollow who has a special bond with a wolf down there."

"Maybe," Braxton said with a nod. "That would make more sense than just a random wolf wondering around."

"Either way, I'm glad he showed himself to us." Lily's eyes lit with excitement. "That's probably a once-in-a-lifetime experience."

"I imagine it is." Braxton felt so connected to Lily in that moment that the urge to reach for her was overwhelming. But instead of taking her hand, he paused and pretended to re-tie his shoe, just to break the spell he was under.

She paused just ahead of him, and once he had himself under control again, he rose. And this time when he joined her, he picked up the pace, needing the day and their time together to be over as soon as possible.

They were all business when they made their way back

into town. After trying out a handful of more food trucks, they made their selections and were able to book enough so that their festival wouldn't be lacking for food options. Then they made their way back to the ferry.

But when they got there, the ticket booth was empty, and a sign had been left on the glass.

Due to the storm, the ferry is canceled. Next run to the mainland is scheduled for tomorrow morning at 8:00.

Braxton blinked at the sign. Then he read it again and let out a curse. "Storm?" He glanced up at the darkening sky and noted that the wind was picking up. "When I looked at the weather report, it called for rain, but it said nothing about a storm."

Lily shrugged. "Sometimes the winds come on quickly. Then she let out a sigh and said, "Well, that's inconvenient. We'd better get to the inn before they run out of rooms."

Inconvenient was an understatement.

But there was nothing else to do. The only way off the island was via the ferry or private boat, and if the ferry wasn't running due to a storm, there most definitely would be a small watercraft advisory.

As he and Lily walked back toward the village, Braxton pulled out his phone and called The Enchanted Outdoors.

"How's your date going?" Dante asked the moment he answered his phone.

Ignoring his friend's taunt, Braxton said, "The ferry stopped running early due to the storm, and we're stuck here on the island for the night. Can you close up and open in the morning? I'll take over once I'm back in town."

Dante let out a bark of laughter. "You're stuck on the

island all night with the girl you've been mooning over for the past month, and you're wasting time calling me? You do realize a quick text would have been sufficient."

"Dante," Braxton said with a warning note in his tone. "Yes or no? Can you do it? If not, just close up early and I'll open when I get back to town."

Lily glanced at him with her brows furrowed.

Braxton shook his head, indicating it was nothing to worry about.

"Relax, Brax. I'm on it," Dante said, sounding exasperated. "Of course, I'll do it. What else do I have going on?"

"I don't know, but I didn't want to assume you were free."

"Even if I did have plans, I'd change them. That's what friends do. Now go enjoy your night with your girl. I'll handle everything here," Dante said.

"I don't have—" Braxton started.

"Bye, Brax. See you tomorrow." The call ended.

He shoved the phone in his pocket and looked up to see Lily staring at him. "That was my assistant. Just letting him know I won't be back until tomorrow."

"I heard," she said, sounding amused as she stopped in front of the Victorian-style inn. "Is there a reason he thinks we're dating?"

Braxton froze. "You heard that?"

She laughed. "Yeah, you might want to turn the volume down on your phone."

"I didn't tell him we're dating. He's making assumptions. Ones I've already tried to disavow. He just won't listen."

Lily pursed her lips and studied him for a long moment. Then she said, "I don't think dating would be so bad. Maybe you shouldn't try so hard to resist the idea." Lily winked at him, pulled the door to the inn open, and disappeared inside.

CHAPTER 7

LILY'S HEART was pounding as she walked into the inn. Had she really just said that? Implied that she'd be more than willing to date Braxton after he'd been running so hot and cold on her?

Guh. What was wrong with her?

She knew the answer. Ever since her grandmother had paired them up to work on the festival, she'd been thoroughly enjoying herself. The fact was that she and Braxton worked well together. And finding out that they both loved hiking… Well, that was just a bonus she hadn't been expecting.

If he'd been any other guy, she'd have just asked him out instead of playing a waiting game. But because he'd bolted after kissing her, not once, but twice, she was determined to wait for him to make the first move. She didn't know if her ego could handle a straight up rejection.

"Hello, welcome to the Waverly Mansion. How can I help you today?" a pleasant woman asked from behind the mahogany check-in counter. Her nametag read *Rita Rosen*.

"Hi, Rita," Lily said, placing her arm on the counter. "I need two rooms for the night."

Rita frowned as she chewed on her bottom lip. "Do you have a reservation, Ms.—"

"Easton. Lily Easton. And unfortunately, no. My friend and I were just over for the day and got caught on the island due to the storm closing down the ferry early. We're happy to take anything you have available."

"Oh, that's too bad. I can't believe how fast the weather rolled in. Last time I looked at the app, it just said possibility of rain. Nothing about high winds and surf advisories." Rita sounded sympathetic as her fingers flew across the keyboard in front of her. Her frown deepened as she looked up and said, "I'm sorry, but there's only one room available for tonight. Would you like to book it?"

The bell above the door chimed, and Lily glanced back to see Braxton entering the inn. He had the same troubled expression on his face that Rita did. "One room isn't going to do it. Are there any other places to stay here on the island?"

"No other inns or hotels, but you can probably find a short-term rental from one of those apps," Rita said. "It's last minute, but I'm sure there's something available."

Lily pulled out her phone, but the minute she tapped the screen, the power went out, plunging them all into darkness.

"Oh, dear," Rita said from behind the counter. The woman quickly lit a candle, giving them a tiny bit of light.

"She only has one room," Lily told Braxton. "I was going to look for a short-term rental here on the island and see if we have better luck that way."

Braxton nodded and pulled out his own phone.

After a few tries to search for one of the short-term rental apps, Lily let out a groan of frustration. "I'm not getting any service."

"Me neither," Braxton said.

"When the power goes out here, the cell towers almost always go down, too," Rita said helpfully. "We'll all likely be without service until the power is restored."

Lily sucked in a sharp breath and looked at Braxton. Their eyes met, and when he shrugged, she turned back around and said, "We'll take the room."

"Can't say I blame you." Rita tapped Lily's information into the laptop she'd produced from under the counter and then wrote down her credit card number. "I'll run this once the power comes back on."

"Sure." Lily glanced around, wondering what she was going to do for a toothbrush.

"Here's the key." Rita reached under the counter and produced two bags. "And here are some complimentary toiletries that should get you through the night."

Lily raised her eyebrows. "Does this happen a lot?"

"More than you'd think. People come over and don't pay attention to the ferry schedule and then get stuck here. Though if you ask me," she said with a wink, "people should get stuck somewhere a little bit remote more often. Everyone is in such a rush these days."

"Can't argue with you there." Lily held up the toiletry bags. "Thanks for this."

"There's a list of nearby restaurants in your room and snacks and refreshments in the refrigerator."

Lily was certain those weren't complimentary, but she appreciated that they were available all the same. "Thank you."

"Let me know if you need anything," Rita called after her.

Braxton took the bags from Lily and said, "Let me know how much the room is, and I'll get you half."

"Not on your life. This one is going to be reimbursed by the event funds. In fact, we should have been keeping the receipts from everything all day. I just forgot about it until now."

"I thought the event was a fundraiser," Braxton said as he opened the door that led to the stairs. Emergency lights at various points on the stairs kept them from being plunged into darkness.

"It is, but Gran doesn't expect us to use our own money to plan the event."

Braxton waved a hand. "I don't mind. Just let me know how much it is, and I'll either reimburse you or stick it in the donation pot."

Lily smiled to herself. He was such a good man, even if he did drive her a little bit crazy. "Put it in the donation pot then. Grandmother would like that."

"Done."

They climbed two sets of stairs before they finally took a right and went to the end of the hall where they found room number 305. Lily used the skeleton key to unlock the door to the most gorgeous room she'd ever seen. A large picture window framed a clear view of the Puget Sound. A few rays of the dwindling late-afternoon sunlight streamed through the darkening clouds, illuminating the choppy water.

Drawn to the window, Lily passed by the queen-size bed that was adorned with a plush comforter and about a dozen pillows. She glanced back at Braxton, who was standing stock-still just inside the door, staring at the bed. Lily wanted to laugh, but instead she just said, "At least we'll have a front row seat to the storm."

"Right," he breathed. "I bet it's a hell of a show."

Lily glanced around at the matching mahogany furniture and then took a seat in an armchair at the desk. "It's pretty early still. If we hadn't eaten our way through the island all day, I'd suggest dinner. Maybe we could get a drink somewhere?"

"Do you think anyone is open?" Braxton asked, already moving toward the door.

"I guess we'll find out." Lily hurried to catch up, and together they went back down the stairs.

Rita appeared behind the desk the moment they stepped into the lobby. "Is everything all right in your room?"

"Yep. It's perfect." Lily said. "We're headed out to see if we can find some drinks. Is there anywhere that might be open?"

"Oh, sure. No doubt Crabby Craig has his doors open.

He prides himself on being the one place people can go when the storms are brewing around here. It's right up the street, maybe two blocks."

"Thanks. I saw it earlier," Braxton said.

It didn't take long to find Crabby Craig's. The freestanding building looked like it hadn't seen any love in decades. White paint was peeling off the siding, leaving the wood exposed to the elements. The roofline sagged on the left side, and the far end of the porch was rotting away. But there were lights on, and the music streaming from the open windows barely drowned out the hum of the generator.

"Looks like an experience," Lily said, praying she wouldn't put her foot through the porch as she climbed the steps.

Braxton let out a huff she took as an agreement.

The outside hadn't been much to speak of, but the moment they stepped inside, Lily couldn't help but feel right at home. The interior of the building was anything but rundown. The old wood floors were solid and freshly stained to match the paneled ceiling. Stunning landscape and wildlife paintings took up most of the space on the walls. And the handsome older bartender was happily chatting away with a couple of locals. Clearly he was in his element, ready to ride out the storm.

"Welcome," the bartender called. "What can I get for you two?"

"What's on tap?" Lily asked.

"All local beers from Westerly Caverns Brewery." He rattled off the different kinds.

"Whichever is the lager," Lily said, taking a seat at the bar.

"Got it." He looked at Braxton, who sat next to Lily. "And for you?"

"The porter."

"Coming right up."

When their beers were ready, Lily held hers up. "To island life."

Braxton snorted, touched his glass to hers, and echoed the toast.

They spent the next hour getting the rundown of the history of the island from the bartender and the two locals until a group of musicians arrived and started setting up on stage. It wasn't long before a bunch more locals arrived, filling the bar.

By the time the guitar player started strumming the first tune, the dance floor was already filled. And when the band launched into "Dreams" by Fleetwood Mac, the crowd went crazy with their approval.

Lily, who was already three beers in, hopped off her chair and tugged Braxton with her. "Come on. We can't skip this."

Braxton reluctantly followed, and when Lily raised her arms in the air and started swaying to the beat, Braxton shook his head, clearly resigned to following her lead, and he swayed with her. They stayed on the dance floor for four more songs, and when the band slowed it down as they played "Silver Springs," Lily was surprised when Braxton immediately pulled her into his arms.

She stared up into his handsome face, lost in the music

and his strong embrace. It was just like the night of the Witches Ball. They'd danced all night, the two of them lost in each other. Being in the arms of Braxton Kirkwood just felt *right*. She couldn't explain it. She'd never felt like that with any other man before. And she just knew that he felt the same. It was written all over his face as he gazed down at her, his eyes locked first on hers and then her mouth.

Lily poked her tongue out, dampening her lips, and noted the flash of desire in his eyes. Her breath caught, and every cell in her body begged to be kissed again. Just one taste.

Suddenly, Braxton pulled away, leaving her skin burning for his touch as he walked out of the bar without saying a word.

Lily fumed and strode after him without a thought, determined to give him a piece of her mind. Once on the street, she spotted him standing at the curb, his hands clasped behind his head as he stared down at his feet. "There's nowhere to run this time, Braxton."

"Nope," he agreed without turning to look at her. "There isn't."

She narrowed her eyes at him. "These mixed signals are getting really old. What is it? Do you have a wife somewhere? A long-distance girlfriend, maybe?"

He snorted and turned around to face her, his expression both frustrated and amused. "If only that was the issue."

"What does that mean? And stop looking at me like that."

"Like what?"

"Like you're doing everything in your power not to carry

me back to that hotel room and strip me naked," she said, hoping to get a rise out of him.

It worked, and he let out a small growl as he stepped closer and yanked her to him. "I'd love nothing better than to do just that, Lily Easton."

"Then what are you waiting for?" she challenged.

"Nothing." Braxton buried one hand in her hair as he tightened his other arm around her waist, pulling her even closer. "Absolutely nothing."

And then he kissed her so thoroughly that Lily's entire world was reduced to the man holding her against his hard frame. His evergreen scent filled her senses, and in that moment, she'd have done anything he asked. Lily clutched at his T-shirt with both hands, wishing the moment would never end.

But time didn't stop, and when Braxton finally pulled away, they were both breathing hard.

"At least you didn't bolt this time," Lily said without looking up at him.

He let out a humorless laugh. "I should. I probably would if there was anywhere to bolt to."

Lily jerked her head up, pure irritation making her skin prickle. "Just tell me why, Braxton. Why do you keep running from this? If you don't have someone waiting for you, I don't get it."

Braxton raised his hand and softly caressed her cheek, regret shining down from his darkened expression. "Because I have to."

"You don't have to do anything, Brax," she railed. "I'm a

big girl. If you're trying to protect my virtue, let me assure you—"

He chuckled, a smile breaking out over his serious features. "It's not that. I'm not quite that chivalrous. It's not you, Lily. It's me." He paused, took a deep breath, and said, "I'm cursed."

CHAPTER 8

"WHAT?" Lily stared up at Braxton, her eyes wide. "What curse?"

Braxton rubbed his hands over his face and grimaced. The rain finally started to fall, and it felt all too fitting considering the grim news he had to share. "It's kind of a long story. Let's go back to the inn, and I'll explain the best I can."

"All right."

Braxton ached to reach for her hand, but he forced himself to keep his distance. He shouldn't have been dancing with her and he sure as hell shouldn't have kissed her again, but the draw had just been too overwhelming. His attraction to her was unlike anything he'd ever experienced before. The only way he was going to be able to resist her was with her help. Once she knew the stakes, he was certain she'd be the one to end whatever was sparking between them.

Lily inched closer to him as they started walking and then slipped her arm through his, huddling closer to him as the wind whipped past them.

He automatically put his arm around her shoulders, trying to shield her from the cold. Everything in him screamed that *this* was right. His soul was somehow aligned with hers, and he had no doubt that, given half a chance, he'd happily spend the rest of his life with her. The thought sent warmth through his chest, but then pain stabbed him just as quickly when he acknowledged that there wouldn't ever be a happily-ever-after in his future.

The rain started to fall harder, and then suddenly there was a crack of lightning followed by a bone-rattling boom of thunder.

Lily jumped and grabbed onto him tighter. He sped up, quickly sweeping her into the inn. Water dripped from their soaked clothes onto the wooden floor, and Braxton gave Rita an apologetic look. "Sorry about that. We got caught in the rain."

Rita waved an unconcerned hand. "Don't worry about it at all. I'll clean this up and then bring you some extra towels."

"Thank you."

Lily started to shiver.

"Is there a possibility of tea?" he asked. "I know the power's still out, but—"

"We have a gas stove. I'll get a kettle going and bring it up as soon as possible," Rita said.

"You're an angel." Braxton smiled gratefully at her before ushering Lily to the stairs.

Once they were back in the room, Braxton activated the flashlight app on his cell phone and led Lily toward the bathroom. She stood just inside the door with her arms wrapped around herself, muttering, "Cold."

"I know." He turned on the shower and was relieved to feel hot water come out of the tap. "Get in the shower and warm up. We'll hang up our clothes so that they can dry."

"What about you?" she asked, the rain still glistening on her eyelashes.

"I'll towel off. It'll be fine." He closed the door behind him and was grateful when Rita knocked on the door a moment later with a fresh stack of towels.

"Tea will be up in a few minutes. Is there anything else I can do for you?" she asked.

"Are there robes somewhere?" he asked, wondering what he'd do if they had to sit around in towels all night.

"Yes, check the armoire. They should be folded up on the middle shelf. There should also be candles in the bottom drawer and battery-operated lights on the nightstands."

"You're a lifesaver." Braxton walked over and pulled the armoire door open. Sure enough, there were two very plush, luxurious-looking robes waiting for him. "Perfect. Thank you very much."

"My pleasure, Mr. Kirkwood." Rita closed the door behind her, leaving Braxton alone in the dark room.

After finding and lighting a half dozen candles, he quickly stripped off his soaked clothes and toweled off before slipping into the larger of the two robes. The soft material felt like heaven after his wet jeans and thin cotton shirt. After hanging his clothes in the empty closet, he grabbed the extra blanket from the top shelf and took a seat in the chair, waiting for Lily.

When the water stopped, he walked over to the bathroom door and knocked softly. "I have a robe for you."

Lily opened the door just a crack and poked her hand out, taking the robe.

Ten minutes later, the tea had arrived and Lily walked out of the bathroom, her cheeks pink and her wet hair fanned over her shoulders. She was so lovely that she nearly took Braxton's breath away. The intimacy of the moment took him by surprise, and he had to look away, feeling as if he were intruding on a private moment.

"Thank goodness Rita was thoughtful enough to stock the bathroom with battery lanterns, otherwise I'd have been fumbling around in the dark." She scanned the candlelit room. "Isn't this romantic?"

"Practical," he said, ignoring the fact that he could have just turned on the battery lights. Was he a glutton for punishment? It appeared so. "Are you done in the bathroom?"

"Sure am. Thank you. I feel a million times better."

"Good. The tea is on the desk." He disappeared into the bathroom, took his own quick shower, and reemerged to find Lily sitting cross-legged on the bed with both hands wrapped around her teacup.

Lily patted the bed beside her. "Okay, we're both cleaned up and warm again. Come over here and tell me about that curse."

He eyed the bed and then looked at the chair. It would definitely be safer to keep his distance.

"Oh, come on, Brax. I'm not going to jump you," she said as she rolled her eyes. "We're friends, right?"

He nodded, though he wasn't worried about her jumping him. He was the one who'd kissed her, all three times. There was no doubt he was the one with impulse control problems.

"Then come over here and tell me what's going on."

How could he say no to that? Braxton grabbed his own cup of tea and then settled on the bed beside her.

Lily placed a light hand on his arm. "I just want you to know that whatever is going on, I'll help in any way I can."

If only. He sucked in a deep breath and said, "Thank you. I appreciate that, but I don't think you can."

She frowned. "I'm sure with the help of my grandmother, we can figure out something."

"Trust me, if you witches have any ideas, I'm all ears. This isn't me being stubborn. But before you start offering help, you'd better hear all the facts."

Lily pulled her hand back, and Braxton instantly felt the loss. It had been a long time since he'd had the comfort of another person's touch. But it wasn't just that he wanted someone's hand on him; he wanted *hers*. She turned, giving him her full attention, and said, "Okay, I'm listening."

"I don't even know where to start," Braxton said with a slight shake of his head.

She gave him a small smile. "From the beginning?"

"I suppose you're right." He glanced down at his teacup. "My family isn't like yours."

"Who's is?" she asked with a laugh. "Three sisters, all witches, and a powerful matriarch witch who's in everyone's business all under the guise of looking out for everyone? I swear, my grandmother is the busiest busybody in the entire town, and everyone just accepts it because she acts like she's royalty or something just because our family were the first witches who came ashore a few centuries ago."

"She might be a little overbearing, but I bet that's mostly felt only by you and your sisters. The rest of us appreciate how much she cares about the town," Braxton said gently.

She shrugged and let out a self-deprecating laugh. "I suppose you're right. I guess it's true that everyone, even the best of families, have some issues."

"Some issues." He let out a huff. "I'd take some issues over"—he waved a hand—"this."

Lily gave him her full attention, and there was no more room for stalling.

"I guess the first thing you should know is that I come from a family of grifters." Braxton watched her carefully to see how she reacted to his confession. When her expression didn't change, he plowed forward. "I grew up in the Florida Keys. Marathon, actually, in a trailer park. My parents were big on scamming rich tourists down in Key West with their snake oil concoctions."

"They sold potions?" Lily asked.

He nodded and ignored the churning in his gut that was always present when he spoke about his family. "Yes. When I was a kid, they made me believe they were all harmless. There were excuses about how it was all just a tourist experience, or people should pay more attention to what they were buying, but later I learned that the potions actually made them more susceptible to suggestion. And my parents were fleecing them."

"Wow, that's terrible."

"It's not even the half of it. When I was eight, my father chose a rich widow as a target and made her believe he was in love with her. He left me and my mother and went off and married her. After only a few months, he managed to gain access to all her assets. Cleaned her out and fled the country. We haven't seen or heard from him since."

Sympathy shone in Lily's eyes as she reached for him again, covering his hand with hers. "I'm sorry, Braxton. I don't know how people can be so incredibly selfish."

"When I was younger, it bothered me a lot," he said honestly. "But now? I wish my mother would have gone with him, and I'd have been free from both of them."

"You're still in contact with your mom?" There was no judgment, just curiosity.

"Unfortunately." He ground his teeth together. There was nothing he wanted more than to change the subject, but Lily deserved to know the truth. "Mom kept up with her potion scams, but when I was a teenager, she got involved with another witch. This one was seriously bad news. He taught her the world of curses. She was a natural, and soon she was a legend in South Florida. People sought her out for all kinds of terrible spells. At first, they were jilted first wives or scorned mistresses. They wanted their exes to be cursed with bad luck in money, love, and especially sex. The amount of erectile dysfunction curses she handed out must have increased the pharmaceutical prescriptions for that little blue pill tenfold."

"It might serve them right," Lily said, though she didn't look amused.

"If only she'd stopped there," Braxton said as he closed his eyes and tried to block out the images of his mother ranting about his father and how if he ever showed his face again she'd find a way to make his life a living hell. "After the man who taught her how to cast all those curses left one day without even a note, she completely lost it. She kept saying she was determined to have just the right spell to punish any man who wronged her in the future. When she wasn't out selling her revenge curses, she spent hours on end in her bunker, testing awful spells. I was in high school by then and stayed away as much as possible."

"I would have too," Lily said quietly.

"The moment I graduated, I was out of there. She went out to scam someone or sell them a curse and I just packed a duffle bag and left. No note. No warning. I just left."

Lily bit down on her bottom lip. "I bet that didn't go over well."

"At first it was great. She had no idea where I was. I'd ditched my phone and got a new one. I was free for about six months, until my college sent something to Dante's house. It was the address I used when I applied. His mom didn't know that I wasn't speaking to my mother, and she dropped it off. That's how my mother found me. Then she showed up at my college and sweet-talked a couple of my friends into letting her into our apartment. I found her sitting in my room, seething. She was angry that I'd left just like my father and told me if I ever cut her off again she'd make sure my life was a living hell. Knowing what I knew about her, I believed her. From that point on, I took her phone calls but did my best to remain as distant as possible."

"I'm sure she didn't make that easy for you," Lily guessed.

"Absolutely not. But I managed to navigate her BS for a while. I saw her when she blew into town. Did my best to keep her out of my life. But when I started dating, she made a point of getting close to my girlfriend, Lucy. My mom would call her, send gifts, and took a general interest in her. I never told Lucy about my troubled past with my parents, but I did warn her that my mother wasn't always on the right side of the law and tried to discourage the relationship. But because she lost her mother to a car accident when she was young, Lucy latched onto my mother and the two became close."

Shaking her head, Lily climbed off the bed and refilled her teacup. "All I see are a ton of red flags. Did she just not care when you warned her about your mother?"

"I'm not sure she really believed me. My mother can be very charming when she wants to be." Braxton rolled his shoulders. "When they started planning a wedding I never agreed to, I broke up with Lucy."

"She didn't take it well, I'm guessing."

"Neither of them did," Braxton confirmed. "My mother was furious. I thought she was just mad because she was losing the daughter she never had, but when everything finally came out, I learned that she had recruited Lucy into her grift. And once we were married, she was going to try to rope me into the scheme, too. Her plan was to use Lucy to get to me. When I learned Lucy was scamming people with those influencer potions, I sent a tip to the Magical Task Force."

Lily's eyes widened and her mouth dropped open into a shocked *O*.

"Yeah. Exactly. Neither of them expected that. Lucy barely escaped a raid and went running back to my mother. The two of them decided I needed to learn a lesson, and that's when Lucy asked my own mother for a curse to bind me to her. Mom was mad that her newest recruit had been burned and could no longer run her scams in our college town, and she agreed to make it for her."

"Your own mother not only allowed her to curse you, but also sold the potion to her, too?" Lily climbed back onto the bed and moved to sit right next to Braxton. "Tell me that she changed her mind. That she didn't do that to her own son."

"Can't. She did it. The curse dooms any relationship I try to have with any woman other than Lucy. Anytime I try to date anyone, terrible things start to happen to them. It's one incident of bad luck after another until I'm out of the picture. The minute I break it off, their lives go back to a normal existence."

Lily narrowed her eyes. "What kind of bad luck? Are we talking acne breakouts or house-burning-down bad luck?"

Braxton lifted his hands, indicating that anything was possible. "The first girlfriend I had after that suffered the most because I didn't know what was happening. She tripped over a neighbor's cat and broke her arm. A day later, she was rear-ended by a garbage truck and her car was totaled. She was the only one out of ten people at her office who got food poisoning at a weekend retreat and spent three days in the bathroom. Her microwave blew up from a supposed power surge that no one else experienced. But the worst was when a sink hole opened up in her front yard, swallowing her and her dog. She emerged with a sprained ankle and a dog who is to this day riddled with anxiety over the event. It was then that Lucy spilled the beans. My girlfriend bolted, and suddenly her bad luck vanished."

"That's horrible."

"Right," Braxton agreed. "And that's why I can't date you, Lily. I won't let my curse affect you that way."

She pursed her lips and studied him. "How together do you have to be with someone for the curse to kick in?"

He shook his head. "I don't really know. Usually all it takes is some flirting and mutual interest for small things to start happening. Bigger stuff usually happens after a few dates. Hard to say. I think it really depends on how much we like each other."

"I see." She placed her hand on his cheek, caressing his five o'clock shadow.

"Lily," he breathed and covered her hand with his. "This really isn't a good idea."

"I think it is. Here's the thing, Brax. I've been into you ever since you kissed me back at the Witches Ball. But so far, I haven't seen even a hint of bad luck. Not unless you count the weather catching up to us and forcing us to stay overnight here on the island. But I have to say, I don't think that was bad luck at all."

"It wasn't," he agreed as he focused on her plump red lips, desperate to taste them again.

"So… What are we waiting for? I'm willing to find out the limits if you are."

He wanted to say yes. He was desperate to throw out all his reservations and pretend he didn't have the curse hanging over his head, but he couldn't. He wouldn't. If anything serious happened to her, he would never forgive himself. Braxton gently pulled away, letting her hand fall to the bed. "I can't. I'm sorry, Lily. I won't risk it."

She let out a long sigh. "I suppose I understand." Sitting back on her heels, she studied him. "You know, it's about time you shed this curse. When we get back to Befana Bay, I'm going to study some of my grandmother's texts and see what we can do about neutralizing it." There was a glint in her eye when she added, "Then we'll see where this thing goes."

Braxton grimaced, hating what he had to say next. "The last person I was interested in tried to do just that, and when she cast her spell, the curse rebounded on her. And now she's in the same boat I am. As much as I'd love to be free of this, it's too risky. I can't let you do that."

"I refuse to believe there's nothing we can do," Lily said stubbornly.

Braxton's eyes started to sting with fatigue, and he laid down on the bed. Staring up at the ceiling, he said, "I appreciate your willingness to help, Lily. But the fact is that I've tried and witnessed the consequences." He rolled over on his side and ran his hand down her arm. "I care about you and your family too much to let you get involved."

Lily looked like she wanted to argue. Instead, she closed her eyes and breathed deeply. When she opened them, she let out a small sigh and then snuggled up next to him, her head on his shoulder. "I hear you, but just so you know, you're not going to stop me from researching this type of curse and any potential cures or reversals."

"I'm not going to change your mind, am I?"

"Nope." She placed her arm over his chest, getting even more comfortable.

Braxton couldn't help it. He wrapped his arm around her shoulder and kissed her on the top of her head. "Research all you want. Just promise me you won't cast any spells."

"I promise I won't cast any spells without talking to you about it first," she amended and then yawned.

It wasn't the answer he'd expected, but it would do... for now.

CHAPTER 9

BRAXTON WOKE with Lily cradled in his arms and the sun warming his face. He blinked his eyes open and studied Lily's relaxed face. She looked so peaceful. Content in a way he hadn't felt in... Well, he didn't know how long. Maybe ever. He wondered what it was like to grow up with a loving family and to have siblings who seemed more like best friends.

The only person he'd ever been able to count on was Dante. And he was grateful. From letting him crash on his couch more times than Braxton could count when they were in high school to being there for him through everything all these years, he couldn't ask for a better friend. But there was no way Dante could fill all the holes in Braxton's tattered soul. No one could.

Growing up with parents who didn't care about anyone but themselves was a nightmare he wouldn't wish on anyone. And although he knew that Lily had suffered her share of hardships, he still would have given anything to have grown up in Befana Bay with three sisters and a grandmother like Bethany Befana.

The longer he laid there with Lily in his arms, the harder she was to let go. There wasn't anything he wanted more than the soft, lovely woman wrapped in his arms. If circumstances were different, he would have already woken her with kisses, and then he'd cover her body with his and claim her in every way a man could.

Every part of his body stiffened, and he had to stifle a groan. His desire for her was overwhelming. If he didn't get out of the bed soon, he'd never leave.

After tucking a lock of hair behind Lily's ear, he leaned down and gently kissed her cheek. Her eyes fluttered momentarily, but then she settled and fell back into her slumber. He smiled to himself, committing the moment to memory. If he couldn't have her, at least he could have this moment.

Carefully, he slid off the bed, grabbed his clothes from the closet, and then locked himself in the bathroom, where he took a cold shower, forcing his body to calm down. When he finally emerged, his skin was icy to the touch, but at least he wasn't vibrating with need any longer.

After he dressed, he found Lily awake and sitting up. Her robe was falling off one shoulder, and her disheveled look nearly drove him insane. Without a word, she walked over to him and placed her hand on his arm. She glanced down. "You're freezing."

"Cold shower," he said softly, barely able to keep from pulling her into his arms. He shouldn't have confided in her the night before. Now he wanted her more than ever. He should have known that baring his secrets to her would only create an intimacy that was irresistible.

She covered both his hands with hers and started rubbing warmth back into them.

Braxton pulled his hands away quickly, afraid he'd cave, and brushed past her to the door. "I'm going downstairs to the restaurant for coffee and breakfast. Meet me there?"

"Uh, sure," she said, looking disappointed. "I'll be just a few minutes."

He nodded and made his escape.

Once he was in the hall, he was able to start breathing again. Was it always going to be like that around her now? Maybe he needed to sell his shop and move to another town. He'd heard Keating Hollow was a nice place to live.

Shaking his head at himself, he took off for the restaurant. Thankfully the storm had died down and the power was back on. After they ate, they could make their way back to Befana Bay, and his time with Lily would come to an end. Sure, he'd still work with her on the Midsummer Festival, but he could insist they meet in public, and he'd have no choice but to keep his hands to himself.

Once seated in the small dining room, he ordered two coffees and breakfast for both of them, confident Lily would be pleased with his choice. If not, she could order something else.

Lily had just taken a seat when their breakfasts came. And once her French toast with a side of berries was placed in front of her, Lily's eyes widened. "How did you know this is my favorite breakfast?"

Braxton shrugged one shoulder and gave her a smug smile. "Lucky guess?"

"Liar," she said without any heat. "Really, how did you know?"

"I have my ways." For months, every Sunday when he walked by the Enchanted Egg Café, a popular brunch spot on the bay, he'd spotted her with French toast. But he wasn't going to tell her that and make himself sound like a stalker. It had been a coincidence the first few times he'd spotted her. Then he'd noted she was always there at the same time, so he started timing his paddleboarding sessions so that he was done just about the time she'd be at the restaurant.

She gave him a skeptical glance, but then once she dug into her breakfast, pure bliss blossomed on her face.

Braxton chuckled. "It's a shame you're not enjoying that at all."

"Right?" she agreed as her gorgeous eyes glittered at him.

"My grandmother used to make French toast for me when I was a kid," he blurted and immediately wished he could stuff the words back into his mouth. Why was he bringing that up?

"Your grandmother? Did you spend a lot of time with her?" Lily asked, putting her fork down.

"No." Sadness washed over Braxton as he thought of the only person who'd ever shown him unconditional love. "She was my father's mother, and she passed a couple years before he took off. But she did come down to our trailer one day a month, and those are my happiest childhood memories."

"Grandmothers, gotta love them," Lily said with a grin, and Braxton was grateful she'd chosen not to pity him.

"Absolutely. But yours is one of the best," he said.

"No argument from me." Lily stabbed another piece of French toast and said, "If you're trying to keep me from falling for you, Braxton, you're going about it all wrong. Without a doubt, French toast is the way into this girl's heart."

Braxton felt his face flush, but then he just shrugged. "I guess my moves aren't all that rusty after all."

Lily let out a huff of laughter. "Definitely not."

CHAPTER 10

LILY FOLLOWED Braxton onto the ferry, disappointed that her time with him was ending. She'd really enjoyed herself over the past twenty-four hours. They'd worked well together while finding the food vendors. She'd known they would. But she hadn't anticipated a walk in the woods. She missed hiking and really hoped he was still up for taking on some trails with her. Though since he kept pulling away from her anytime she got close, she wasn't holding her breath.

But she could hardly blame him. Not only was the man cursed, but it was because of a potion made by his own mother. Talk about trust and abandonment issues. Braxton had to have them in spades. If she'd been in his shoes, she'd have stopped dating, too. She couldn't imagine being responsible for all the terrible things that had happened to the women he'd been interested in.

But none of them were descendants of Bethany Befana,

the most powerful witch west of the Mississippi. No matter what Braxton said, it wasn't going to stop her from trying to help him. It wasn't just because she was drawn to him either. No one deserved to have to live in constant fear that if they got close to someone they'd be hurt. It was beyond cruel.

Lily didn't know if she was powerful enough to break such a curse, but no doubt the collective power of her family could tackle it. She'd have to do her research first, of course, but then she'd find a way to get Braxton his life back.

"Inside or outside?" Brax asked her.

"Inside. It's still a little cool after yesterday's storm."

He nodded and led them to the same seats they'd occupied the day before.

Lily sat across from him and pulled out her notebook. "When are you available to go check out some bands?"

He jerked his head up. "You want to go together?"

"Yes," she said patiently, understanding his hesitation now. "It's not a date. Don't worry. I won't jump you or anything."

"I should be so lucky," he said so quietly she almost didn't hear him.

Why did he have to keep flirting with her? If he expected her to keep her distance, he was going to have to knock it off. Though she knew why. He wanted her just as much as she wanted him. And as much as he wanted to deny himself, knowing that she was willing even after he'd explained his curse meant she was driving him crazy.

Good.

Because she was going to come out of her skin if she kept having to deny the fireworks going off between them.

"The store closes at six, so I can go any night. We probably need to do that sooner rather than later," he said.

Lily pulled out her phone and checked the calendars of a couple local bars. "Does tonight work? There are a few bands playing around here that I like."

He narrowed his eyes at her. "If you're already familiar with them, why do we need to check them out?"

Busted. She'd just wanted an excuse to spend time with him. The truth was she already knew who she wanted to hire. "Don't you want a say?"

He shrugged. "If you like them, I'm sure they'll be fine."

Frowning, she sent off an email to the band she liked, asking if they were available to play the event. When there was an almost immediate reply, she had to stifle a sigh. "Looks like Midnight Mage is in. You're off the hook."

"Maybe I'll go check them out anyway," he said as he stared out at the water.

Lily smiled to herself, already planning her outfit.

"There you are!" a woman cried as she stomped over to them.

Lily and Braxton both startled as they turned to the short, slim woman. Her curly ash-blond hair was piled up on her head in a messy bun, and she wore leggings and an oversized sweatshirt with a Westerly Island logo on it.

"How dare you stand me up for this… this *girl*." The woman waved a hand at Lily with a look of disgust on her face.

"I'm sorry," Braxton said, glancing from the woman to Lily and back again. "Do I know you?"

The woman let out a gasp as she clutched her chest with one hand and covered her eyes with the other. "I just can't believe you'd do this to me. *Again*. Don't you love me anymore? Have you *ever* loved me?"

"Brax?" Lily asked. "Who is this?"

He shook his head, looking panicked. "I have no idea."

"Now you're pretending you don't even know me? After all I've given up for you? After putting up with all your lying and cheating and broken promises?" Tears rolled down the woman's cheeks. "I should have known you were out with one of your side pieces. You'll never change." She buried her face in her hands, and her shoulders shook as she cried silently.

Other passengers on the ferry were staring, and Lily had no idea what to do or what to even think. Was this woman one of Braxton's exes? It didn't seem like it. She clearly seemed to think they were still dating. But Braxton didn't. He didn't even appear to know this person. One of them was lying, but Lily was too confused and shocked to make heads or tails of the dynamic.

"I just can't believe this is happening," the woman whimpered. "Not again."

Braxton finally seemed to shake himself out of his stunned state. He stood and moved over to the woman. "Ma'am—"

"Ma'am?" she cried, staring up at him, her face red with anger. "You called me *ma'am*? How dare you?" She launched herself at him, beating on his chest with both fists.

Braxton raised his hands up in a surrender motion, trying to take a step back, but he was blocked by a row of seating.

Lily jumped up and grabbed the woman by the shoulders, pulling her back from Braxton. No matter what had happened, violence wasn't the answer.

The woman immediately froze and stood there, looking around as if she didn't have a clue where she was. "What…" She cleared her throat and then looked at Braxton, her expression turning to one of horror. "Oh no. I don't—I'm sorry." She shook her head, trying to stumble away from Lily, but Lily still had her hand on her arm, stopping her.

"Hold on," Lily said. "How do you know Braxton?"

The woman shook her head. "I—I don't. I don't think so anyway." She lifted her head and gave Braxton a pained look. "I'm sorry. I don't know what happened."

Braxton swore under his breath. "It's the curse."

Lily felt a cold dread slither through her body. Was that true? If so, why was some random stranger affected?

"Curse?" the woman asked as confusion clearly mixed with fear in her trembling limbs and wide eyes.

Lily turned her attention back to the woman. "What's your name?"

"Pia. I'm sorry. I don't know what came over me. This…" She waved a hand between herself and Braxton. "This isn't a thing. I don't even know this man." Then she peered at Lily. "But I know you."

Lily raised her eyebrows in surprise. "You do? How?"

"You're that woman who writes that "Ask Endora" column, aren't you?"

"Yes," Lily said with a slow nod. The memory of the woman flashing Braxton in front of his store ran through her mind, and dread formed a ball in the pit of her stomach. She didn't really want to know, but she had to ask. "Have you read my column lately?"

She nodded. "Yes. That's what I was doing before..." Pia chewed on her bottom lip as realization seemed to dawn in her eyes. "Oh my gosh."

"What is it?" Lily and Braxton asked at the same time.

Lily couldn't shake the feeling that her column had something to do with the woman's outburst, but she hadn't advised anyone to verbally attack a stranger. Not that she could remember anyway. Her head started to pound. All she knew was that something had come over Pia, and she was almost certain it had to do with Braxton's curse.

"I have to get it. Hold on." The woman twisted out of Lily's hold and took off for the other side of the ferry.

Lily and Braxton glanced at each other and then followed close on her heels.

"Here it is." Pia pulled an old issue of the *Befana Bay Bulletin* out of a tote bag and handed it to Lily.

The date was from almost two years ago. Lily scanned it and felt her blood run cold. The letter was asking what to do about a cheating husband, and Lily's sarcastic advice was to confront them both in a public place and make the biggest, most embarrassing scene possible. At the end, she followed it up by saying the sensible thing to do was to talk to her partner and decide if there was anything left to save in their marriage, and then she suggested individual or couple's marriage counseling.

Braxton gently pulled the paper out of Lily's hands and read the column. When he was done, he handed it back to the woman and apologized.

"Oh, no. I'm the one who should be apologizing," she said, sounding earnest. "I just don't know what came over me." She let out a humorless laugh. "Maybe I'm finally losing it."

"You're not. Trust me," Braxton said. "It's me. I'm cursed." Then he grabbed Lily's hand and hauled her away from the woman. "He called back over his shoulder. "Maybe just stop reading 'Ask Endora' for a while."

Lily hated to admit it, but he was right. That was twice now that people had taken her satirical advice and made fools of themselves when it came to Braxton, and it was all Lily's fault. She'd have to stop writing her column until they found a way to break the curse.

An announcement sounded over the intercom that it was time to disembark. Lily was surprised to see that everyone else had already moved to the front of the ferry. She hadn't even noticed them docking.

"This is my fault," Lily said as they made their way off the boat.

"No, it isn't. It's my mother's fault." His voice was low and full of anger.

"Okay, I'll give you that. But I'm going to fix this. Mark my words, Braxton Kirkwood; I will not let some vindictive witch ruin your life or mine."

Braxton stopped suddenly and looked down at her. "All you need to do is stay away from me. Once that happens, everything will go back to normal."

"You think so?" she asked, her voice defiant. "Even if that's true, what about you? Are you really going to live the rest of your life this way? Denying yourself happiness because of the effed-up crap your mother has heaped on you? I know you've been burned before, Braxton, but I'm not going to give up. You can tell me to mind my own business, but as far as I'm concerned, this *is* my business. *You* are my business."

She knew it was a little bit crazy to be making such a declaration when they hadn't even spent that much time together, but she wasn't delusional in thinking there was something real between them. The curse proved that. If they didn't have feelings for each other, then none of this would be happening.

Braxton just stared at her for a long moment. Then he pressed his lips together in a tight line and shook his head. "I didn't tell you about the woman I dated who owned a bakery, did I?"

"No." Jealousy climbed up her throat, but Lily swallowed it down. She didn't want to hear about his other girlfriends, even though she already knew they'd all ended in disaster.

"We dated a bit before I really understood what was happening with the curse. By the third date, everything had started to go wrong at her bakery. The oven died. The freezer went out. The point-of-sale system imploded. The entire staff came down with some mysterious flu. When the toilet blew up and spewed raw sewage everywhere, that's when I finally realized the shit had hit the fan. When she refused to break up because she didn't believe me, a life-sized ceramic pig literally fell out of the sky and smashed through the roof of her bakery."

"What?" Lily cried. "A flying pig? How is that even possible?"

"The city was doing some demolition, and someone got a little carried away with the explosives. That's not the point though. Don't you see? If we keep this up, the consequences are only going to get worse."

"Okay, fine," Lily said. "I get it. You're a walking disaster. You've accepted it, but I haven't, and I think it's time to fight back. One way or another, I'm going to figure out how to give you your life back."

Something soft and tender flashed in his blue eyes, making Lily want to wrap her arms around him and make sure he knew he wasn't alone in this. But then his expression hardened, and he said, "Don't say I didn't warn you." Then he walked off, leaving her standing there at the ferry landing.

"I'm going to fix this," she called after him. "And when I do, I expect a date of epic proportions."

She heard him snort, but he didn't look back.

With determination in her heart, she headed home, ready to get to work.

CHAPTER 11

THE EVENING AIR was cool on Braxton's face as he climbed out of his truck. It was dusk and he was just getting home after spending the day at his store, catching up on paperwork he'd had left over from the day before. Dante could handle the customers and the point-of-sale system, but he hadn't yet been trained on closing out the receipts and preparing the banking deposits.

The day had been a nice one with the sun out and a very light breeze, which meant a steady stream of business. He'd skipped lunch and hadn't had a thing to eat since his breakfast with Lily that morning.

Lily.

He'd tried not to think about her all day. That had been a hard task to accomplish after her declaration that morning. It was far too tempting to imagine a life where he was free of his curse and was able to dive into a relationship with her. But he'd been down that path before. He'd once had all the hope and determination she did, but in the end, he'd just been left broken and still cursed.

Braxton prayed for her sake that she'd give up on her mission sooner rather than later. It would kill him to see her life in shambles because of him, even if it was something he couldn't control, no matter how much he wanted to.

A light shone from his front window, indicating that Dante was home, though he didn't see his friend's SUV anywhere. Braxton briefly wondered if he'd just forgotten to turn the light off when he'd left.

Walking in, he tossed his keys in the bowl on the table by the front door and headed straight for the kitchen. It wasn't until he heard the creak of the swivel chair in the living room that he paused and turned around, expecting to see Dante.

The small woman with bright red hair and rings on every finger was decidedly not his best friend.

Braxton froze, his entire body rigid with tension. "What are you doing here?"

"Now, baby, is that any way to greet your mother?" she said, pasting on a sickeningly sweet smile.

"I could have started with get the hell out. Is that better?" He crossed his arms over his chest and glared at her. "In case I wasn't clear, you're not welcome here."

His mother's smile crumpled, and tears filled her big green eyes.

Braxton was not moved. He'd witnessed Katerina Kirkwood turn on the waterworks more times than he could count. It was one of her best moves when she was trying to break down someone's defenses.

"Now, don't be like that, honey." She stood and walked over to him, and he noticed she looked thinner than usual. Her skin was unusually pale, and there was a hole in her tights that she wore under her brightly colored print skirt. Something was wrong, and he wondered if her life of crime was finally catching up with her. "I walked past your store today. It really is lovely. I always knew you'd make something of yourself."

A muscle in his jaw ticked. "You're not welcome there either. If you're here because you think the store is making me rich, you should just move on now. It's a new business, and I'm up to my eyeballs in debt. There's nothing to squeeze out of me. Go find another mark."

It was a lie. The truth was that the store had started to make a profit almost immediately. Befana Bay was a town that thrived because of the film industry. There were at least two shows that filmed there regularly as well as a rotating schedule of movies. Hollywood types loved Befana Bay due to the magical shield that kept paparazzi out of their town. It made it much easier to control the media narrative since they could release what they wanted the public to know instead of having to always respond to invasive photos and gossip. With Hollywood money always infiltrating the town, it made owning a shop there a solid business plan.

"I'm not here for anything to do with your store," she said, sounding frustrated. "Listen, honey, I know you're still mad at me, and you have every reason to be. I'm not denying that. I'm here to right my wrongs. Make it up to you. Start over. You know, be the mother you always deserved instead of the one you got."

Was Braxton hearing things? Who was this person standing in front of him? Sure, he'd witnessed her lie year after year, cry when needed, and make up pretty much any story to get what she wanted, but he'd never once heard her admit that she was a bad mother. Or that she'd been wrong to curse him. The last time he'd confronted her, she'd said he got what he deserved for abandoning Lucy and turning her in to the authorities. That all men were dirt, and he had to pay for the sins of his father.

With bad memory after bad memory plaguing him, he walked over to the front door and held it open. "You should leave."

The tears she'd been holding back streamed down her face.

Braxton remained indifferent to her emotions.

"I've given up the grifter life," she said through a sob.

"Why?" he asked, unable to contain his intense curiosity. He figured there was a less-than-zero chance that she was telling the truth. She knew there was no way he'd let her stay with him while she was running scams, and there was also a high likelihood that everything coming out of her mouth was a lie.

"About a month ago, I had a brush with the law. The person I was with was taken into custody. He was caught red-handed, and there's no doubt he'll serve serious time. He wasn't a good person, Brax." She rubbed at her arm as if soothing an ache. "When I realized I was free of him, I had an epiphany of sorts. I realized that if I didn't get out of that life, I was likely going to wind up in prison. Either that or I'd end up with someone else just like him, and I just... I can't. I won't survive it. I want to get out of the life."

"And you thought this was the best place to come?" he asked incredulously. "You think I'm going to help you after everything that's gone down between us?"

"You're the only person I know who isn't in the life," she pleaded. "Please, Braxton, if you help me, I'll reverse your curse. You'll have your life back. I swear."

Her words froze him in place. He nearly stopped breathing as a tiny thread of hope wound its way around his heart. Lily's smiling face flashed in his mind, and in that moment, he felt he'd do just about anything to have a chance with her.

Anything but believe his conniving mother.

"You told me you couldn't reverse it. That you tried and failed."

"I lied," she said, her voice meek. "I was angry, baby. You'd turned on me, and I lashed out."

He wanted to believe her. He was desperate to, but he'd been burned too many times. "Why should I believe you now? You've lied to everyone your entire life. How do I know you aren't making that up just to get me to go along with whatever you have cooked up now?" He took a deep breath and continued before she could answer. "If you were really sincere, you'd reverse the curse first. You wouldn't be asking for anything in return."

"I would. I swear, baby." Her panic was even more pronounced as she started shaking, and Braxton had to reluctantly admit that he'd never seen her quite like this before. "It's just that I need to either find Lucy to help with the curse, or I need to team up with a powerful coven. I can't do either of those things if I'm struggling to find housing and my next meal. I swear, if you let me stay, the first thing I'll do is work on reversing that curse. All I need is a place to sleep and a good meal or two. I swear, no scams, no bullshit. This is just me trying to do something right for a change."

Braxton stared at her, trying to see past the mess of a woman in front of him and deep into her soul. Could he trust her? The answer was decidedly no. But the temptation of being free of the curse was just too much for him to deny.

His mother stared at the floor, a sure sign of defeat. Did she think he was going to say no? It sure looked like it, and it was on the tip of his tongue to do exactly that. But then he thought of Lily. If all that was at stake was his desire for her, then he'd be able to slam the door in his mother's face. But it wasn't. Lily was determined to help him, which put her right in the line of fire.

"You can stay in the apartment above the garage," he finally said.

Her head popped up, her eyes full of surprise. "Really?"

"Yes, but if you don't get started working on this curse right away, or if you do anything that even remotely looks like you're grifting again, I'll have you run out of this town so fast it'll feel like your ass is on fire. Got it?"

She held her hand up. "Got it. I promise. No more selling shady potions or curses or anything like that. I'll find a job somewhere in town and pay rent just so you know I'm not trying to take advantage of you."

"Reverse the curse first, then we can talk about rent." He

gestured for her to head back out the front door. Then he showed her to the small garage apartment. "It isn't much, but it has a wall heater, a bathroom, and a small kitchen."

"It's perfect," she said.

It wasn't. The linoleum was peeling in the kitchen, there were hard water stains in the sink, and the walls looked like they hadn't been painted in twenty years. But it was better than sleeping under a bridge.

"I'll bring you some dinner later," he said as he was leaving.

"I can come make us something," she said, sounding hopeful.

He turned around, gave her a flat stare, and said, "No. I don't think we're ready for that. And for the record, you're not welcome in the house. You can stay here, but if I find you digging through the house, all bets are off. Got it?"

"I suppose I deserve that," she said. "I understand."

He gave her a quick nod and then closed the door softly behind him. Braxton stood at the top of the apartment stairs and felt his entire body sag with fatigue as he wondered what he'd just done.

CHAPTER 12

"Gran?" Lily called out as she walked into the large Victorian two days after her impromptu overnight stay on Westerly Island. "Are you here?"

Bethany Befana appeared in the foyer, a bundle of herbs in her hands. "Lily? Did I know you were coming over today?"

"No." Lily chuckled as she walked over and gave her a hug. "I just dropped in. Wanted to do some research in your library and pick your brain a little."

"Okay, give me about fifteen minutes. I'm working on my energy clearing bundles. They are almost ready for the spell to be cast."

"Take your time," Lily said as she climbed the stairs to the second floor. Lily had gone straight home the day before and spent most of her time going through online archives from the Salem Witches Library, trying to find a way to reverse the curse for Braxton. But she hadn't found anything useful. She had a sneaking suspicion that the curse she was looking for was restricted. As it should be. It was highly illegal to use a curse that dangerous.

Light streamed through the open window of the library, illuminating the rich dark wood. And when the breeze blew in, the sheer curtain billowed, making it look like something out of a fantasy novel. With bookcases filled from floor to ceiling on each wall, the room was a researcher's dream.

Lily walked over to the section that was labeled research only and found books on illegal black magic, curses, and hexes. She'd never spent any time going through these tomes. There'd never been any reason to. Without a search engine or card catalog, the task seemed daunting. But she was determined, so the only thing to do was to start opening books. She went through five fairly quickly, dismissing them due to the grim topic of sacrifice. Braxton's mother didn't sound like the type to do anything that would cost her anything as precious as her power.

Lily switched bookcases and thought she might have hit paydirt. All the curses in that section revolved around revenge of the heart. She pulled out five of the books and sat at the big desk that was situated right in the middle of the room. After flipping through two of them, her stomach roiled. The things people were willing to do to each other sickened her. There was everything from wiping someone's memory to cursing them to being loveless for the rest of their lives.

When she spotted the curse to magically bind someone to another person against their will, she stopped and read the pages more carefully. It didn't look like the exact curse that had been cast on Braxton, but it certainly was similar. If the person tried to form a connection to someone else, bad things started to happen. Only this one was specifically designed to make a person sick if they strayed. Vomiting, headaches, and hives appeared to be the most common issues.

Lily put that book aside with a marker at that page and picked up another book. By the time her grandmother walked into the room, she was ready to burn all the books.

"We shouldn't have these just lying around," Lily said, slamming the book shut.

"They aren't just 'lying around,' Lily. You know that," Bethany said patiently. "If anyone who isn't a Befana were to walk in here, they'd be trapped near that door and stuck until one of us came and released them. No one is getting access to the books here without permission."

"I suppose, but they just seem so... accessible. Like we're asking for trouble just having these books out in the open." Lily couldn't shake the horrible feelings she'd gotten while going through the curses. She just could not understand why humans had to hurt each other. It made her stomach churn.

Bethany rubbed her granddaughter's shoulders. "Tell me what you're looking for. Maybe I can help."

Lily picked up the book she'd set aside and opened it to her marked page. "I'm looking for a curse very similar to this one, but the particulars are a little different." She went on to tell her grandmother about Braxton's curse and the women who'd been compelled by her articles to act out her advice on him.

"Oh dear," Bethany said. "No wonder he had such dark energy. I bet it's already tainted again," she mused. Then she looked at Lily. "Or maybe not if he's been spending time with you."

"What does that mean?" Lily asked, frowning.

"Just that you have very pure energy, and it would affect his in a positive way." She gripped one of the crystals she was wearing around her neck as she studied the curse in the book. "You're right. This doesn't sound like the exact curse that's been cast on Braxton. But I do think I know which one it might be." She tapped her lips with one finger as she studied the bookcase. After a moment, she closed her eyes and chanted a finding spell in Latin. When she pointed her finger at the bookcase, one on the far end on the bottom shelf illuminated as if glowing from within the pages. "There it is. Grab that one for us, honey."

Lily did as she was told and handed the book to her grandmother.

Bethany opened the book immediately to the correct page and started to read. "Destruction of the Heart Curse is meant to bind one person to another for life, and if they harbor feelings for someone else, unfortunate events will keep occurring until that person is no longer a threat." There was a long list of possible incidents, but then at the bottom of the page it said the consequences would manifest as something specific to the person who had come between the two people who were bound together.

"That sounds exactly like it. No two people experienced the same issues." Lily told her grandmother about Braxton's exes and their bad luck and then said, "So far, the only thing that's happened to me is that people are acting out the satirical advice in my columns and taking it out on Braxton. While none of that is devastating, it *is* humiliating for the women and Brax. The only side effect for me personally is a desire to censor myself so that no one does anything particularly awful."

Bethany nodded. "I suspect it hasn't escalated because you're a Befana witch. Your powers are strong enough to keep that curse at bay. So it's found a way to affect those around you, but not you personally."

Lily let out a huff of frustration. "So if I keep seeing Braxton, anything that I've written could potentially be acted out by random people of Befana Bay?"

"Looks like it," she said, sounding sympathetic. "I know that's frustrating, but at least no one will have ceramic pigs falling from the sky."

"There is that, I suppose," Lily said, sitting back in the chair and silently hating Braxton's mother. "How do we neutralize it?"

"Looks like the best way is to find the person Braxton was bound to, and then a spell can be cast to break the curse."

"What if she can't be found? Is there another way?"

Bethany frowned at the book as her brows knitted. "There is a way, but it's very unpredictable. If it goes wrong, the spell rebounds onto whoever has feelings for Braxton." She looked down at her granddaughter. "That's you. It's too risky, Lily. You could end up cursed just like Braxton."

"But Befana Bay has a powerful coven. They could help, right? Surely a curse like this isn't too much for them."

"It's a lot to ask, Lily. If the curse rebounds, it won't be just you who is affected. You'll bear the consequences, but then all my friends and I will have to live with the fact that we caused that harm. You know what that does to a witch over time."

Causing harm eroded powers as well as compassion, and all of the Befana Bay witches were particularly wary of abusing their powers. It had happened before. They refused to let it happen again. "I know, but can we at least ask them?"

"We will at the next coven meeting." Bethany slammed the book closed and put it back on its shelf. "Now, let's go get some tea and cleanse our energy. We don't want any negativity sticking to us after going through all those curses."

"Sounds perfect to me."

ONCE LILY WAS BACK HOME, she went onto her back porch with her notebook, took a seat in the wooden swing, and called Braxton.

"Hey, you," Braxton said after the first ring. "What's up?"

"I need to know Lucy's last name," she said, getting right to the point.

When he answered, his tone was hesitant. "Do I want to know why you're asking?"

Lily chuckled. "Probably not. Should I tell you anyway?"

"You're trying to find her, aren't you?" He sounded

frustrated, and she wondered if she was stepping over the line.

"Are you okay?" she asked. "If you really don't want me to do this, just tell me and I'll back off, but—"

"It's not that," he said, letting out a deep breath. "My mother showed up last night."

"The one who sold your ex a curse?" She winced and wished she could shove the words back down her throat.

"That's the one. Katerina Kirkwood is now staying in my garage apartment. She says she's here to make amends, to break the curse, but I don't know if I believe her."

Lily whistled softly. "That's big news. What made her show up now?"

"I have no idea. She says she's out of the grifting and cursing business and needs a place to get back on her feet. If it wasn't for the curse, I'd slam the door in her face, but I just... couldn't. If there's even a possibility she's telling the truth, I have to see this through."

"I don't blame you," Lily said, but she had a bad feeling about it. Scammers rarely changed. "But how about you give me Lucy's last name, and I'll work on finding her, too. That way maybe we'll find her before your mom crosses your boundaries."

He let out a soft chuckle. "That sounds like a plan. It's Lansing. Lucy Lansing."

Lily scribbled it down in her notebook. "I'll do everything I can. In the meantime, what can I do to help?"

"Tell me I'm not crazy for letting her stay?"

"You're not crazy," Lily said with conviction. "Anyone would do the same in your shoes."

"I don't know about that, but thank you for saying so."

They chatted for a few more minutes before Lily said, "Okay, I'm going to start working on this. Call me if you need anything."

"I will. Goodnight, Lily."

"Goodnight."

Lily ended the call and sat back, wishing that she'd asked Braxton to come over. She'd like nothing more than to feel his arms around her again. She closed her eyes, imagining how things would be different if he wasn't cursed and then put her fantasies aside and got to work.

She pulled up her contacts on her phone and tapped the screen.

As the phone rang, she got up and paced the back deck.

"Lily, long time no chat," Ressa said when she answered.

"It's been a while since we've had to do any background checks," Lily said. "How are you?"

"Not bad. I was thinking of heading out to Befana Bay for the Midsummer Festival. I heard it's pretty good."

"It's fantastic. Though, I might be biased since I'm in charge of planning it this year," Lily said with a small chuckle. "You should come, though. I'd love to see you."

"I will. Now, why did you really call? 'Cause I know you didn't ring my phone just to ask how I'm doing. And if I'm not mistaken, there isn't any filming going on in your lovely little village at the moment either. Everyone's on a break, right?"

"You're right on both counts. I need a favor. It's a personal one."

"I can certainly try. Hit me," Ressa said.

"I need you to find someone for me. A grifter, one who isn't afraid of using illegal curses. Can you do that for me?"

"Sure. If they're traceable, I'll find them. Text me the name and any other information you have on them. I'll start a trace tonight."

"You're the best," Lily said, feeling relieved to finally be doing something. "I owe you one."

"Only a beer when I see you at the festival." Ressa clicked off, and Lily got busy texting her the details.

Fifteen minutes later, Lily climbed into her tub with a glass of wine in hand, wishing a certain tall dark and handsome outdoor shop owner was there to share her bath with her.

When her phone rang, she grabbed it and was only slightly disappointed to see it was her sister Indigo. "Hey, what's up?"

"Dinner. That's what's up. The four of us are meeting up in an hour to eat at The Salt Circle. Then we're going for drinks. We're not taking no for an answer."

"When did you decide this?" Lily asked, staring down at the bubbles in the water.

"Five minutes ago. Gran says you need girl time. So be there, or we're coming to drag you out of the house."

Lily laughed, suddenly feeling lighter. Her grandmother always knew what she needed. "No need to drag me out. I'll be there with bells on."

"Good. And wear something dangerous. It's ladies' night at the bar." The call ended, and Lily hauled herself out of the bath and got busy looking her best.

CHAPTER 13

"Can I speak to the manager please?" a familiar voice said from behind Braxton. He dropped the inventory sheet and turned, a huge smile claiming his lips. "Niko? What the hell are you doing here?" He hurried out from behind the counter and pulled his childhood friend in for a tight hug.

"Looking for a kayak," Niko said when he pulled back, his face lit with amusement. "What else would I be doing here?"

"That's a long way to come from Florida just to get a kayak," Braxton joked. "Seriously, what brings you here to Befana Bay?"

Niko ran a hand through his dark curls and glanced away for a moment before he said, "I needed a change of scenery, and I figured what better place to go other than where my two best buddies are."

The weight of Braxton's troubles seemed to melt away as he stared at the friend he hadn't seen in over fifteen years.

He, Niko, and Dante had all been friends in high school, but once Braxton and Dante went away to college and Niko moved to Key West to join his uncle's charter boat business, their lives had gone in opposite directions. And for some reason, they hadn't found time to visit. "I just can't believe you're here," Braxton said. "Have you seen Dante yet?"

"Not yet." Niko gave him a smug smile. "I literally just rolled into town."

"How long are you staying?" Braxton was already mentally trying to juggle his schedule so that he could make time to spend with Niko.

"A while."

"What the hell does that mean?" Braxton asked with a laugh as he led Niko through the store. "Are we talking a couple of days? A week maybe?"

"I leased a short-term rental for a month, so at least that long. Maybe more. We'll see."

Braxton stopped abruptly and turned to look at his friend. "A month, maybe more? Seriously?"

"Seriously."

"What about your charter business?" Braxton asked. Niko had taken it over from his uncle when he'd retired a few years earlier, and summer was his peak season. "Did you hire someone to run it?"

"Nah. It's closed. Like I said, I needed a change of scenery. This was my first stop." He glanced over at the bay. "Maybe I'll open a new charter business here. I don't know yet. I'm still thinking things over."

"Whoa, that is a big change," Braxton said, wondering what had prompted the move. Instead of prying, he said, "If you're looking for something in the meantime, we could use someone to manage our kayak tours."

Interest lit Niko's gaze. "Really?"

"Yeah. The guy who did it last season moved out of state, so we have an opening. It's yours if you want it."

"I'll think about it."

"You do that." Braxton clapped him on the shoulder.

"Hey," Niko said suddenly, "I ran into your mother on my way here. I thought you two weren't talking? What's she doing up here?"

Braxton swallowed a groan and then forced himself to say, "She's turning over a new leaf or something."

"Sounds sketchy," Niko said and then added, "I know she's your mom, but keep your guard up around her, okay, man? After the shit she pulled when you were a kid…"

He didn't need to finish the sentence. Braxton knew all too well that he was right. "Don't worry about it. That trust was broken a long time ago."

"Niko?" Dante called just in time, saving Braxton from his least favorite topic of conversation. "Hey, man, how the hell are you?"

They embraced and Braxton quickly caught him up on the little information he'd pried out of their friend.

"This is incredible, man," Dante said. "I can't believe you didn't let us know. We have to make plans immediately. What's it been, fourteen, fifteen years? We have a lot of catching up to do."

"Fifteen," Braxton said.

Dante put his arm around Niko and pulled him in for a sideways hug. "Tonight, the party is on."

"It better be. I hauled my ass all the way across the country to see you two," Niko teased. "But first, we have plans."

"We do?" Braxton asked. "When?"

"Right after you close this place down for the night." Niko glanced at his watch. "Which is in about five minutes, right?"

"Yes," Dante answered for Brax.

"Good. Meet me out front." He turned and walked out of the store, leaving Dante and Braxton behind.

"You really didn't know he was coming?" Dante asked Brax.

"Nope. No idea." They'd spoken on the phone every month or so for years, but life had gotten complicated for all of them, and getting together just hadn't worked out. "It's really great to see him though."

"It really is," Dante agreed.

The pair got busy shutting the store down, and when they stepped out of the shop, Braxton took one look at Niko and the enchanted broomsticks lined up against the building and let out a loud laugh. "I should have known this was what you'd planned."

"Broomstick races. Classic. What are the stakes?" Dante asked.

"He who comes in third has to buy all the beers tonight. Second buys food. First basks in the glory of knowing he's the king of broomstick racing," Niko declared. "Agreed?"

"I'm in," Braxton said.

"Hell, yeah." Dante walked over and grabbed one of the brooms.

"One last thing," Niko said. "These are rented from Brooms that Vroom, and if you break it, you buy it."

"Then don't get crazy like you did with those spelled skateboards," Dante added.

"Or the enchanted BMX bikes," Braxton chimed in.

Niko threw his head back and laughed. "Damn, I missed you guys."

They each mounted their brooms as Niko said, "The only rules are to fly to that shipping marker, then around that water tower, and then land back here on this sidewalk. Got it?"

"Got it," Brax and Dante said at the same time. "On three?"

Niko counted down, and the three of them took off like rockets over the water, nudging each other to jockey for position. Braxton found himself in the middle, getting squeezed by them both, but when he pulled up on the front of his broom, he shot upward and the pair of them crashed together. He leaned forward and shot into the lead, cackling like he was fifteen years old again and having the time of his life with his two best buddies.

Braxton was just circling the shipping marker when he was buzzed by Dante. "Hey!" He leaned forward, sending his own broom darting forward. But when he felt the wind shift, he looked up and spotted Niko right above him, waving as he shot ahead of him.

"Dammit!" he cried and held on with both hands, willing his broom to go faster. But no matter what he did, his broom seemed to lag behind. And when he rounded the water tower, he felt like he was riding on one cylinder instead of six. His buddies were ahead of him, battling it out for first place, each of them knocking the other in the shoulder hard enough to throw their opponent off course.

Braxton watched with amusement as they twisted and spun, clearly having the time of their lives as his broom puttered along, obviously in need of a serious tune-up. Finally, Niko glanced behind them and pulled up short when he spotted Braxton's broom struggling. He turned his attention back to Dante and held up his hand in a stop motion. They flew close together, no longer fighting for position, and then suddenly they both turned around and flew right toward Brax.

For a second, Braxton was sure they were going to unseat him. But instead, they split off and came up along either side of him.

"No man left behind," Niko said as he and Dante both held an arm out for him. "Grab hold. We'll get you back before you plunge into the sea."

"I'm not going to plunge into the sea," Braxton said, glancing down. Right? He really didn't think so. The broom was having issues but...

The broom sputtered, and sparks shot from the handle. It wobbled, and Braxton immediately grabbed his two buddies and wrapped his legs around the broom to keep from losing it. "I think maybe you were right."

"Hold on!" Niko said as he and Dante guided him back to the store. The three of them landed awkwardly, causing Braxton to fall to the sidewalk. He laid there for a long moment and then started to laugh. It was the kind of laughter that took over his entire body, making him shake with amusement.

"You think he's okay?" Niko asked Dante.

"Definitely. I think this is just a little stress reliever. It's good for him."

Niko looked concerned. "What's he stressing over?"

"The usual. His mom. His girl. The crazy women who keep coming onto him with their outlandish tactics," Dante said as if Niko was supposed to know what all of that meant.

Through his laughter attack, Braxton heard music start to play. As it got closer, he sat up and groaned when he recognized the song "In Your Eyes" by Peter Gabriel. He scrambled to his feet and stared in horror as a woman in a trench coat crossed the street holding a boom box over her head.

"Would this be Brax's girl or one of the crazy women?" Niko asked Dante.

"One of the crazy women," Dante said with an incredulous smile. "I don't know what it is about him that's got all these women vying for his attention. He's not that good looking, is he?"

"Definitely not," Niko said. "How often does this happen?"

"This is the third," Braxton said. "Come on, let's get out of here." But the moment he tried to walk away, the woman jumped into his path and held up a sign that said, "Are You Free Friday Night?"

The three men stared at her in astonishment, and Braxton said, "I'm sorry, but I'm not."

The woman just dropped her sign, turned the volume up on her boom box, and started twerking.

Finally Braxton cleared his throat and said, "Wasn't this a facetious suggestion in an 'Ask Endora' column earlier this month?"

Both of his friends indicated they had no idea. But Braxton was certain he was right. This was the advice in Lily's article, and he had to admit that as embarrassing as it was, it could have been worse.

Braxton wasn't paying any attention as he called Lily. The moment she answered, he said, "It's happening again."

"Is that 'In Your Eyes' playing?" she asked.

"Yes. Boom box. Strange dancing. Any of this ringing a bell?" he said into the phone.

"I'm on my way." A moment later, Brax saw Lily burst out of The Salt Circle and run over to the strange woman.

The moment Lily placed her hand on the woman's arm, the woman stopped her dancing, blinked, and then stood upright and looked around. "What's happening?" the woman asked.

Lily whispered something to her. During their conversation the woman nodded and then looked over at Braxton, horrified. She glanced once at her boom box, but instead of grabbing it, she just shook her head and hurried off to a red Toyota Camry. As the woman was speeding down the street, Lily's sisters exited The Salt Circle and stood on the sidewalk watching as she went to talk to Braxton.

"Hey," she said as she looked down at the broom and

Braxton's scuffed elbow. "What happened? Did you crash when you saw your stalker?"

"No. That happened before she showed up."

Lily's lips twitched with amusement, and suddenly she started laughing. She laughed so hard that tears started running down her cheeks.

Dante and Niko joined in, but Braxton wasn't amused. They weren't the ones who were being stalked by twerking randos.

"I'm sorry," Lily gasped out. "But the twerking. It was funny when I wrote it, but to see it live..." She wheezed and clutched at his arm, holding herself steady. "I really am sorry. It was better than being bitched out on the ferry, though, right? I've suspended my article for the time being, so there's less chance of this happening, but there's nothing I can do about past articles. At least this one was funny instead of tragic."

Braxton felt his tense body start to relax, and eventually he smiled at her. Even he had to admit that the twerking had been on another level. "I suppose I should be thanking you."

"You don't need to. That visual was quite enough." She smirked and then looked over at Dante and then Niko. As she focused on the newcomer, she held out her hand and said, "Hi, I'm Lily. I don't think we've met."

"We most certainly haven't," Niko said, giving her an approving glance. "I'd have remembered."

"Careful," Dante warned. "That's Brax's girl you're trying to flirt with."

Braxton took that opportunity to wrap his arm around

Lily's shoulders and pull her in closer to him. After dropping a kiss on the top of her head, he said, "Thank you for coming."

She gazed up at him, her expression full of surprise. "Anytime."

He knew he'd been giving her mixed signals, but he was just tired of trying to stay away from her. If he was going to be embarrassed on the daily due to her columns, he might as well let himself enjoy his time when he was with her.

"What are you and your sisters doing tonight?" Dante asked. "Are you up for a few beers?"

Lily grinned at him. "Well, it just so happens we were headed for the bar ourselves." She turned her attention to Braxton. "Should we join you?"

"Definitely," Dante said before Braxton could answer.

Brax gave him an irritated look and then turned his attention back to Lily. "I'd love it if you could join us."

Lily patted his chest just over his heart and leaned into him as she waved her sisters over.

CHAPTER 14

LILY GRINNED AT HER SISTERS. "Looks like we have dates to the bar tonight."

Sage laughed. "I'm sure August will be pleased to learn that.

"Call him and have him meet us," Lily urged and then introduced Prim, Sage, and Indigo.

When Niko took Indigo's hand, she gave him a half smile and said, "Well, I didn't expect to see you here in Befana Bay. You're not stalking me, are you?"

"No, but if I'd known you were here, I just might have come sooner." He lifted her hand and pressed a kiss to her palm, "It's lovely to see you again, Indigo."

"Uh, explain?" Lily demanded. "When did this happen?"

"Maybe they had a salacious rendezvous when he was renting those broomsticks," Prim said with a giggle as Indigo proceeded to ignore them.

Niko glanced at the broomsticks. "Do you work at Brooms That Vroom?"

"She owns it," Braxton said.

Niko chuckled. "Isn't that interesting? It looks like the universe is really invested in us meeting again, doesn't it?"

Indigo rolled her eyes. "All you had to do was call if you want a date. You don't have to involve the universe."

"Now I know." He held his arm out to her. Indigo slipped her arm through his, and the pair headed up the street, leaving everyone behind.

Lily turned to her sisters. "Did you know anything about this?"

Both Sage and Prim shook their heads.

She glanced at Braxton. "How about you? Did you know they knew each other?"

"Nope. I haven't seen Niko since high school. We didn't even know he was coming to town until he showed up today."

Lily peered after them. "Indigo has some serious explaining to do."

Sage chuckled and said, "Let's go get our drink on. Once Indigo has a few in her, I bet we get the story we're looking for."

The unlikely group headed to The Grimoire, the town's newest fancy bar. One entire wall was filled with spell books while the other was lined with various top-shelf liquor bottles. It had an upscale vibe with mood lighting, fancy leather chairs, and gorgeous hardwood tables. It was a perfect atmosphere for the magical town of Befana Bay.

"I love this place," Lily said as they found a long table

near the back where they could all sit together. She started to pull a chair out, but when Braxton moved to the other side of the table to sit next to Dante, she quickly changed course and plopped down right next to him. When he shook his head at her, she just smiled and said, "Get used to it, buddy. If another victim from my column shows up, I'm the only one who can snap them out of their trance, so my plan is to stick as close to you as possible."

"So I'm supposed to think of you as a shield?" he asked, looking amused.

"Exactly." She leaned in, gently bumping his shoulder.

"And what if something worse happens? What if the curse starts targeting you?"

Lily sobered and stared into his eyes. "Then we'll cross that bridge when we come to it. In the meantime, can't we just enjoy what we have? Because Brax, the thing is, the curse isn't going away as long as I have feelings for you. Pushing me away isn't going to change anything."

A swarm of emotions flashed through his dark eyes, and as much as Lily loved her sisters and was happy to be spending time with his friends, she wished with all her heart that they were alone so that she could show him just how much she cared for him.

Finally, Brax put his arm around her shoulders and gave her a soft, lingering kiss before he whispered, "Okay."

"Looks like I missed a few things," August said, drawing Lily's attention.

She smiled sheepishly at her sister's partner and said, "That's what you get for spending all your time in your studio."

Sage laughed. "Yeah, I used to be the workaholic. Looks like we switched rolls. He's been hiding away in his studio all month."

August rolled his eyes. "That's not true. Though I do admit that I've been spending more time there these days. What can I say? When the paintbrush calls, you do what you have to do."

"After that painting of Levi and Silas was featured in the local paper, it made the rounds with the celebrities, and now he's inundated with commissions." Sage pursed her lips and gave him a side-eye glance. "And he's had trouble saying no."

"What can I say?" He laughed. "It's nice being wanted."

Lily chuckled. "I bet. Plus, you needed inventory for the Midsummer Festival."

"Also true," August said. He and Sage had neighboring booths, and even though Sage was needling him, she didn't really have room to talk. Lily happened to know that she was putting in some extra hours to make sure she had a full range of stock as well. And this time her grandmother hadn't given her a hard time about it. Lily supposed since Sage actually was making time for her boyfriend and her sisters, Bethany wasn't as bothered by Sage's workaholic tendencies.

There was an uproar of laughter from the other end of the table, and they all turned their attention to Indigo, who was challenging Niko to a broomstick race.

"Just tell me the time and place, Easton," Niko said, his eyes flashing with defiance. "You don't scare me."

She raised one eyebrow and said, "You sure about that? I

hold the record for fastest flyer in the nation. I wouldn't blame you if you wanted to bow out to save your ego from being crushed, but if you want to get your ass kicked, I'm all in."

Niko's lips twitched with amusement. "How about we make it interesting?"

"Oh, you want to place a bet?" Her eyes sparkled, and Lily couldn't remember the last time she saw her older sister look so radiant. There was something about Niko that really lit her up.

"Is it even a race if there aren't any stakes?" he asked, holding her gaze. The way they were looking at each other, Lily wondered if they even remembered there were other people in the room.

"If I win," Indigo said, "I want that romantic candlelit dinner we never got, followed by dancing under the moonlight just like you promised down in the Keys."

"Keys?" Lily whispered to Sage. "Did you know Indigo went to the Keys?"

Sage nodded. "Yeah. It was when she went to that enchanted retreat a couple of years ago after the busy season so she could recharge."

That sounded vaguely familiar to Lily. It had been around the time she'd been under deadline for an "Ask Endora" anthology. "Recharge?" she said with a laugh. "Sounds like whatever happened down there, it definitely worked. Though I'd envisioned a spa retreat with salt scrubs and facials, not a hot weekend with some random stranger."

Sage cackled. "Sounds like whatever happened, she had a

lot more fun than she would have if she'd spent the entire time in the steam room."

"I bet there was plenty of steam," Lily mused.

They both started giggling while Braxton and August got up to head to the bar.

Prim cleared her throat and gave her sisters a disapproving shake of her head. "Maybe you two shouldn't be talking about this with Indigo sitting right there."

"Oh, Prim," Lily said. "She's not even paying attention to us. Look at her. She's only got eyes and ears for the new hottie in town."

Prim glanced at Indigo and Niko and bit down on her bottom lip.

"What is it?" Sage asked her.

"I don't know. Something just feels off to me."

"About Niko?" Lily was on full alert. Prim had a sense about people, an intuition that was almost always on target. If she thought someone was bad news, it was time to sit up and take notice.

"No." She frowned. "I mean, not about his character or anything. It just… I don't know. It just feels like everything isn't as it seems. I can't really explain it."

Lily focused on Niko. There was no denying his charm, and she could see why Indigo was so into him. But it was strange that he just showed up unannounced after he and Indigo had some sort of connection from a couple years before, and now he and his best friends were in Befana Bay. It was all just a little too coincidental.

When Braxton returned, Lily asked, "How did you end up in Befana Bay?"

He blinked at her and then said, "I was looking for a fresh start and mentioned it to Niko during one of our monthly calls. He said if he ever left Florida, he was considering Befana Bay. I looked it up, and now here we are."

Lily, Sage, and Prim all shared a look. Didn't that just explain it all.

"You don't know what you're talking about," Indigo said, her voice raised as she challenged Niko. "I'm telling you, some of the best-written books out there are cozy mysteries."

He scoffed. "You're telling me they're better than suspense?"

"Absolutely. You just get more with a cozy mystery. Family, friendship, community, and a murder to solve. With suspense, usually it's just one or two people on their own, trying to just survive. I'm not saying they are bad, but who wants to read about a life like that all the time?"

"Clearly, a lot of people," Niko said with a smile as he continued to challenge her. "Just look at the bestseller lists. There's no denying they are popular."

Indigo rolled her eyes. "Yeah, for people with cold, dead hearts." Then she rummaged around in her bag and pulled out a tattered copy of *Louisiana Longshot*, a book by Jana DeLeon. "Read this and tell me it isn't some of the best writing and storytelling you've ever read in the mystery genre."

Niko picked it up, read the description on the back, and said, "I'll give it a shot if you do something for me."

She raised one eyebrow. "What?"

Without a word, he slipped his hand into her hair and pulled her in close, their lips a mere inch apart. "Let me take you home tonight."

Everyone was silent as they waited for her answer.

Finally, Indigo seemed to realize that everyone at the table was staring at them. She pushed him away and said, "Nice try, suspense boy. Read the book, and then we'll talk."

He laughed. "Okay. But what about that broomstick race?"

"Oh, we're still doing that," she said. "Tomorrow. Then we'll decide when you're taking me on that date."

"Or when you're cooking me that homemade meal," he countered and then winked as she flushed pink.

CHAPTER 15

"Can I walk you home?" Braxton asked Lily as they all filed out of The Grimoire.

She took stock of her sisters. Prim was sticking close to Indigo, while Sage had already said her goodbyes and was headed home with August.

When Niko said goodnight and headed toward his SUV, and Indigo and Prim took off in the other direction, she said, "Yes. I'd like that."

Dante waved as he got into his own vehicle, and suddenly it was just the two of them.

Braxton wrapped his arm around her shoulders and pulled her in close as he steered her toward her house. But she pointed to the waterfront and said, "Let's take a bit of a detour."

He nodded, and she leaned into him, letting out a contented sigh. Everything about him just felt right. Natural.

"I like you like this," he said.

"I like me like this too." She looked out at the bay and the silver moon reflecting off the water, so contented she couldn't imagine living anywhere else. "I've lived here my entire life, and nights like this still take my breath away. How is it possible for a place to be so beautiful?"

"It really is something special," he said as he stared down at her, and she got the distinct impression he wasn't just talking about the landscape. "I guess I owe Niko a huge thank you. If he hadn't mentioned Befana Bay, I never would have ended up here."

"Can I ask you something?" Lily asked as she paused near the dock that led down to the boats.

"Sure. Anything."

"What's the deal with your friend Niko?"

He raised both eyebrows, appearing surprised by her question. "What do you mean?"

She pressed her lips together, not sure what to say. "I don't know. I guess I just want to make sure my sister isn't walking into something she can't handle."

He chuckled softly. "It looks to me like Indigo can handle just about anything. In fact, none of you Easton girls are exactly shrinking violets."

That got a laugh out of her. "True." But then she sobered. "It's just that Prim felt like something was off. She said she felt like not everything was as it seems with him, and I don't want Indigo to get hurt if Niko has a wife or someone back in Florida waiting for him."

Braxton released her shoulder and took her hand in his

as he led her over to a bench and tugged her down to sit next to him. He stared down at their entwined fingers and said, "I can't say for certain that there's no one waiting for him. It's been a while since we talked. It feels like his current plans are pretty up in the air, so maybe that's what Prim is picking up on. I am willing to go on record to say that Niko is a standup guy, and even though I haven't seen him in a long time, I still believe that's the case."

"People change. You can't know that," she reasoned.

"You're right. People do change. I have. But we all have secrets and pasts. That's just life. Are you telling me that Prim didn't have reservations about me?" he challenged.

Lily laughed. "She told me you were a lost cause and that I should date one of the rotating actors that breeze in and out of town so that I could at least make some connections and get a movie deal out of my column."

He stared at her incredulously. "Really? That seems very callous for Prim."

Lily waved an unconcerned hand. "She was joking. The last thing Prim would do is advocate for any one of us to date an actor."

"Why's that?"

"We're married to this town. Most actors are only here temporarily. If any one of us talked about leaving, I'm not sure what Prim would do. Probably knife a tire to keep us in town longer," she said with a chuckle. "Seriously, family is everything to her and has been since our parents died. It would be very hard on her if one of us moved away."

"I envy that," he said, caressing her cheek. "The closest

I've come to having a real family is Dante. And to a lesser extent, Niko."

"Found family is just as important," Lily said. "It's why I'm determined to help you break that curse. Because, Braxton?"

"Yeah?" he breathed.

"I'm fairly certain that no matter what happens going forward, you're a part of mine."

His eyes closed for a long moment as he let out a long sigh, and then when he opened them, he took her cheeks in both hands and kissed her.

Lily leaned into the kiss, parting her lips for him. His tongue tangled with hers, and the entire world vanished, leaving only Braxton and the way he made her feel when he was holding her. They kissed for so long that when they finally came up for air they were both breathless.

Braxton touched his forehead to hers and said, "I should probably get you home."

She wanted to say that she *was* home. That being in his arms made her feel safe and secure. But she kept it to herself and nodded, letting him lead her up the hill to her small cottage.

When they got to her front door, she started to invite him in, but he kissed her one last time and said, "I'll talk to you tomorrow."

She stood with her hand on the doorhandle, watching him go, knowing that they'd had a breakthrough, and everything had changed. She just prayed it was for the better.

LILY WAS STARING at a blank computer screen, daydreaming about the kiss the night before, when her phone rang, startling her out of her thoughts. She glanced down and saw Ressa's name pop up on the screen and hurried to answer it. "Ressa, have you got something for me?"

"Sure do. Are you ready for this?"

Lily scrambled to open her notebook and grabbed a pen. "Yep."

"Lucy Lansing's last known address is in Hansville, Washington."

"Hansville?" Lily gasped out. "You're not serious. That's like twenty miles from here."

"Very serious. I found an alias attached to her, Maryse Madyson. That name with her same birthday was filed on a lease agreement with the county two months ago. There's not much out there on her from the past six to eight years. I found one address in Tucson, but nothing else. She's been very careful about staying underground, but these days, with everything online and security cameras everywhere, it's harder and harder to do."

"What in the hell is she doing in Hansville?" A ball of unease formed in her gut. She knew on a cellular level that Lucy was in Washington because of Braxton. But why now, after years of being MIA? It was more than a little suspicious that both Braxton's mom and Lucy were now in Washington. Were they working together against Brax again? She could barely stomach the thought.

"Lily?" Ressa asked. "You still there?"

"Yeah. I'm here. Give me the address. I think it's time to find out exactly what Ms. Madyson is up to."

Ressa gave her the information and then said, "Be careful, Lil. There's usually a very good reason that people go off grid like that."

Lily sucked in a breath and said, "I know, and I will. Thank you."

The minute she ended her call with Ressa, Lily called Prim.

"What's up?" her sister asked after the first ring.

"Are you busy? I need someone to ride along with me to Hansville."

"I can probably get out of here for an hour or two. Viv is working with me today. What's in Hansville?"

"Braxton's ex," Lily said, her voice full of venom.

"The one who cursed him?" her sister gasped out.

"The very same."

"I'll be right over," Prim said.

Lily ended the call and went to put on jeans and a plain T-shirt. Something that wasn't too identifying. If she got a chance to talk to Lucy, she wanted to fly under the radar.

Two minutes later, Lily's door flew open and Prim burst in. She was wearing a pretty red dress with a colorful crocheted cardigan over it. Lily took one look at her and shoved her into her bedroom. "You can't go like that."

Prim looked down at herself. "Why? I think I look cute today."

"You do. Especially for a yarn shop owner. But not when we're staking out Braxton's ex. Here." She shoved a pair of jeans and a long-sleeved shirt at her, knowing her sister always ran cold.

"Fine," Prim said with a sigh. "But I'm going to need shoes, too."

"Already on it." Lily handed her socks and a pair of tennis shoes. "I'll be waiting in the car."

When Prim was dressed, she jumped into the passenger seat of Lily's car and said, "I didn't realize we were going undercover. Should we stop for some masks, too?" she asked sarcastically.

Lily glanced at her. "Funny. I just don't want to stick out if we do run into her. I figured we could pretend to be new neighbors. Find out what her story is, why she's here."

"If she's here for Braxton, you don't think she'd tell the truth, do you?"

"She might. I hear that criminals try to stick to the truth as much as possible so they don't get caught in a lie." Lily handed her the address Ressa had given her. "Will you set up the navigation?"

"Sure. Worth a shot then." Prim sat back in the car and tapped the address into her GPS.

Twenty minutes later, they drove past a small blue home with an overgrown lawn and dead potted plants on the porch, though the house itself looked as if it had been well maintained. There wasn't a car in the driveway, nor were there any signs of life.

"Doesn't look very promising," Prim said.

Lily drove past a few more houses and then turned onto another street and parked her car. As she pushed the door open, she said, "Come on. Let's go investigate."

"What are we going to do, break in?"

"Of course not. Though if a door was left open, I wouldn't be opposed to just checking to make sure there are no dead bodies."

Prim groaned. "I can't believe you just said that out loud. You do realize we are like ninety percent likelier to find an actual body now, right?"

"That's just a superstition. Now come on."

"Superstitions are a thing for a reason, Lily. You know that as well as I do."

"Either way, I'm still going to investigate with or without you."

Grumbling to herself, Prim fell into step beside her sister and said an audible prayer to the goddess of life to protect them from any lingering spirits.

"Good one," Lily said. "I would have forgotten all about that."

"This is why I'm here. I keep you out of trouble."

Lily nodded. "Yep. It's why I didn't call Indigo. She'd have already barreled in and likely tripped some sort of booby trap."

They both laughed, knowing that was an over-exaggeration even if there was a kernel of truth to it. Indigo was the most impulsive of the four sisters.

When they got to the house, Lily walked right up the driveway and onto the porch.

"What are you doing?" Prim asked.

"Finding out if anyone is home." Lily knocked on the door. When no one answered, she hit the doorbell and listened carefully. "Did it ring?" she asked her sister.

Prim nodded.

"Good. Looks like she's not here. There's no dog either." Lily glanced around at the neighborhood. The houses were a good distance apart. Hansville was fairly rural, and that worked in Lily's favor. "You stay here as a lookout. I'm going to go around back and see if anyone is back there."

"You're going to go see if the back door is open," Prim said, her tone dripping with disapproval.

"What you don't know won't hurt you," Lily said as she walked off the porch.

"It will if I get arrested."

Lily pretended she didn't hear her sister. So far, they hadn't done anything even remotely illegal. The weeds along the side of the house were even thicker than they were in front, and Lily started to doubt that Lucy was even staying at the house. Though she supposed there were plenty of renters who were terrible at lawn and yard care.

The backyard was just as deserted as the front, and Lily didn't hesitate to walk up onto the back porch and peer into the kitchen window. She spotted a mug and a dirty pan in the sink. A loaf of bread was sitting on the counter along with a plate of butter. Someone was living there. They just weren't home.

After glancing around again, Lily grabbed the doorknob and twisted.

Locked.

"Damn," she muttered and then checked the windows. Every single one was closed and locked. There'd be no breaking in today. Not unless she wanted to bust out a window, but even that was too far for her to go. She took one last look in another window and spotted an open suitcase with a pile of clothes on the floor. The bed was mussed, and a pile of cosmetics were visible on the dresser. It was enough to confirm that a woman was staying there, but since she hadn't fully unpacked, it made Lily conclude it was likely a temporary stay.

"Did you find anything worth going to jail over?" Prim asked when Lily met her back in the front of the house.

"Chill out. It's not like I picked any locks or busted through a window." She led Prim back down the driveway as she filled her in on what she saw.

"Didn't you say she signed a lease two months ago?" Prim asked.

"That's what Ressa said. Maybe she rented it in advance and just got here? Or maybe she's anticipating a quick getaway?"

"Or maybe she's just a slob and has been too lazy to unpack," Prim mused.

"I guess any of that is possible. Do you have to get back right away?"

Prim shook her head. "Not unless Viv texts to say we've suddenly gotten busy."

"Good. I want to do a stakeout to see if Lucy comes home anytime soon."

As they climbed back into Lily's car, Prim said, "I knew we should have brought snacks."

Lily laughed and opened the middle console, revealing a bag of sour cream and onion potato chips and a package of Red Vines. "Will this do?"

"You're incredible. You know that, right?" Prim said with a smile.

Lily nodded and handed the Red Vines to her sister, knowing they were her favorites. Then she moved her car so that they were parked down and across the street from Lucy's house, but they still had a decent view of both the driveway and the front porch.

They sat in the back seat of the car so they'd be hidden by the tinted windows, munching on snacks for almost a half hour before a black Ford Bronco with a rental tag on the back pulled into the driveway.

Lily sat up at full attention, her phone camera ready to go. She wanted pictures of Lucy so she could show Brax and make sure it was the same woman.

But when the door of the Bronco opened, a man in black pants, a tight black T-shirt, and a black baseball cap jumped out. He pulled the ball cap down low, obscuring his face as he walked up to the front door.

"That's definitely not Lucy," Prim said.

"He doesn't live there either," Lily said as they watched him knock and then peer through the front window.

Prim glanced at her sister. "Looks like we're not the only ones looking for Lucy Lansing."

Lily peered out the window. "Am I crazy, or is there's something familiar about that guy?"

"How can you tell?" Prim asked, studying him. "All I see is a man in a black uniform."

"One who is scoping out the place exactly like I did an hour ago," Lily said as she watched him take off to the back of the house.

Prim let out a breath. "I suppose this is what happens when one lives their life grifting and scamming people. How often do you think she runs from people like him?"

"I don't even want to know," Lily said.

After about twenty minutes, the man reappeared and headed for his truck. They still couldn't see his face, but when he pulled the door open, the wind picked up and blew his cap off. Prim let out a gasp. "That's Niko!"

Lily leaned forward, squinting at the man in question, and she felt her heart get caught in her throat. Prim was right. It was Niko. What the hell was he doing snooping around Lucy's place? Had they been in cahoots all these years? Or was he there trying to help Braxton just like she and Prim were? If he was helping Braxton, wouldn't he have just told him that instead of being vague and insisting he needed a change of scenery?

"I told you there was something off about him!" Prim cried. "Follow him."

Lily scrambled into the front seat and waited until Niko pulled out and was turning right at the end of the street before she stepped on the gas. When they made the turn, she followed at a good distance for about a mile before she spotted him turning into the small parking lot of a neighborhood coffee shop.

"Go over there," Prim instructed, pointing to a beach access parking lot across the street. The sun had started to shine, and there were a handful of cars in the lot, making it a good place to stop.

They pulled in next to a minivan and waited. And waited some more while Niko disappeared into the coffee shop.

When he reappeared, he had a coffee cup in one hand and his phone in the other, pressed to his ear. And then, as if he had some sort of unnatural radar, he looked up and peered right at Lily. His eyes narrowed as he ended his call and walked across the street, straight toward her.

"Oh hell," she breathed.

"How did he do that?" Prim asked.

But Lily didn't have time to answer before there was a loud knock on her window.

Even though she knew he was coming, she still jumped and then let out a nervous laugh as she rolled the window down. "Niko!" she said, acting surprised. "What are you doing out here today?"

"I was just about to ask you the same thing," he said casually. "I was just checking out a house that's scheduled to be auctioned and getting the lay of the land to see what I think of the area. And then I stopped for coffee. What about you?" He peered into the car and spotted Prim in the back seat. "Everything okay?"

"Of course," Lily said. "We're just out tracking the whales." She tapped her phone. "Last we heard, they were headed up this way from Kingston. We're hoping to get a sighting, maybe a few pictures. It's something we do every now and then when they're in the area."

He blinked, and she wondered if he believed her. If he didn't, he did a good job of masking his skepticism. "Really? I'd love to see that. Any idea how far away they are?"

Crap. "Not sure. Prim, do you know?"

She felt her sister kick her seat as she said, "I'm not sure either. I'm not getting great cell service right now, so I'm having trouble tracking them. Last I heard they were headed north, but you know how it goes. Sometimes they abruptly turn around to hunt. Tracking the orcas is so unpredictable."

"I bet," he said. "Well, maybe I'll stick around and see if they turn up."

Lily swallowed as she looked back at her sister, pleading with her to say something. If Niko knew anything about Befana Bay, he already knew that the orcas visited the bay almost every morning, and it was unusual for the residents to try to track them down along the rest of the shores of the Salish sea.

"Oh dear," Prim said. "That's Viv texting." She waved her phone. "Looks like she needs me back at the yarn shop in Befana Bay."

Lily gave Niko an apologetic smile. "Darn, looks like we have to run. Good luck catching sight of the whales. Let us know if you find them." She put the car into gear and eased out of the parking lot, leaving Niko in their dust.

"We have to tell Indigo that there's something up with him," Prim said.

"Yeah, but what? That he was snooping around Lucy's house, just like we were?"

"I don't buy it. He looked more like a cat burglar," she said. "And what was that about when he came over to us? He must have realized we'd followed him, but he didn't call us out on it. Why?"

"I don't know. What do you think about his claim that the house is scheduled to be auctioned?" Lily asked, feeling more confused than ever. Niko had just shown up in town the day before, and already he was snooping around Lucy's rented house. She didn't know what to make of it.

"Seems like an excuse to me," Prim said.

Lily made a mental note to check the county website and see if his story checked out. "What if he was just trying to find Lucy so he could help Braxton?" The idea wasn't out of the question. Niko was one of Braxton's best friends. Lily knew she'd do just about anything for her sisters, the women she thought of as her best friends.

"No way." Prim sounded almost incredulous over the idea. "I'd be more inclined to believe he's tangled up in something with Lucy. He hasn't even seen Braxton in over a decade. You aren't going to convince me that he's suddenly interested in helping Braxton sort out his personal life."

"You have a point," Lily said, slumping over her steering wheel as she waited at a light. "We need more information about Niko. That's all there is to it."

"What are you thinking? A background check?" Prim asked, looking pleased at the idea.

"Maybe. I want to talk to Braxton first."

"Bad idea." Prim shook her head. "He's only going to defend his friend. We need more evidence that Niko is up to something before you take this to Braxton."

Lily groaned, knowing her sister probably had a point. But the idea of keeping Braxton in the dark made her stomach ache. They were just starting their relationship. Keeping secrets and telling lies of omission wouldn't do them any favors. "I still think I need to tell him. If Niko is involved with Lucy somehow, it's better he knows now rather than later when he's caught off guard."

"So you're going to tell Braxton about Lucy's house, too?"

Lily nodded. "As soon as we get back to town."

"Okay," Prim said, brushing her hair back and into a ponytail. "But don't say I didn't warn you."

"There's no chance of that."

CHAPTER 16

"Spill it," Dante said with a grin as he leaned against the checkout counter at The Enchanted Outdoors.

"Spill what?" Braxton said without looking up from his clipboard, though he knew exactly what his friend wanted. That was too bad for him because Braxton wasn't interested in sharing.

"What is going on with you and the feisty blonde? What happened last night?"

Braxton looked up at his friend and gave him a flat stare. "I don't kiss and tell."

"Ah-ha!" Dante threw his fist in the air as if he'd won something. "So there was kissing at least."

"No comment." Braxton walked out from behind the counter and headed to the break room. It was midafternoon, and he needed a shot of caffeine to keep him going.

"Dude. That's all I'm getting?" Dante sounded disappointed.

"There's nothing to tell. I walked her home, and that's it," Braxton finally relented.

Dante studied him for a long moment. "Considering your past behavior of swearing off relationships, I'd say it's a hell of a lot more than nothing."

Braxton would too, but he wasn't interested in analyzing it. He'd come to terms with the fact that there was something between him and Lily, and he wasn't willing to ignore it. If he thought about it too much, he was afraid he'd talk himself out of spending time with her. That was the last thing he wanted.

"Fine," Dante huffed. "I can take a hint. But just know that I think she's great for you, and if you mess it up you're an idiot."

"I'm well aware of that last point," Braxton said and gave his friend a self-deprecating smile.

The front doorbell chimed, and they both returned to the front of the store. A woman wearing a low-cut dress that showed off all her best assets walked wright up to Braxton and ran her hand down his arm. She gave him a warm smile and said, "Braxton Kirkwood, you're just the man I was looking for."

He glanced down at her hand and then took a step back, putting a little space between them. Clearing his throat, he said, "What can I help you with today?"

The woman let out a tinkling laugh. "You don't remember me, do you? We met a few weeks ago at the bookstore. I was looking for a cookbook, while you were looking at the home improvement section."

He frowned. That sounded vaguely familiar, but he didn't remember having much of a conversation with her.

"Let me refresh your memory. I'm Mallory, and you said you loved shortbread cookies." She opened the tote bag she was carrying and handed him a plastic bowl. "So I tried a new recipe. I thought you might want to try them."

He eyed the bowl, noted it was full of shortbread, and smiled at her. "That's very kind."

She stepped so close to him that he could feel her breath on his cheek. "Why don't you come over tonight and we can discuss them."

"Uh, that's a kind offer, but I'm afraid I can't." He backpedaled, placed the bowl of cookies on the counter, and typed out a quick text to Lily.

The woman continued to follow him around the store, making excuses to touch him and flirt with him for the next ten minutes. Even when Dante tried to distract her, the woman was relentless.

It wasn't until Lily walked in, made a beeline for the woman, and placed a soft hand on her shoulder that the woman finally came out of her trance. She quickly apologized and left, her face flaming red.

Braxton sighed. "Thank you." He wished he had some way of warding off unwanted advances other than using Lily as a human shield, but short of throwing someone out of the store, he just didn't know what that might be. And he certainly didn't want to use force on someone who was being compelled to act a certain way because of a curse. He just wasn't sure how to handle it all. Maybe he just needed to spend as much time with Lily as possible. His heartbeat sped up, and he decided that was an excellent idea.

"No problem," Lily said. "I was already on my way over. Do you have a minute to talk?"

"Okay, seriously. What is going on?" Dante demanded. "What was that all about? This isn't the first time some woman has thrown herself at you like she was under some sort of spell. And now I just watched Lily single-handedly send her on her way without so much as a word. I'm not crazy, right? Was that woman under a spell?"

Lily glanced at Braxton with her eyebrows raised.

He groaned and glanced around to make sure there weren't any customers in the store before he turned to his friend. "Yes, she was under a spell. And Lily here is the only one who seems to be able to interrupt the cycle."

"What spell?" Dante asked.

"Lucy wasn't happy when we broke it off, and she bought a curse from my mom to bind me to her. Now every time I date anyone, things go haywire. This time, women seem to be taking Lily's satirical advice literally and using it on me."

Dante just stared at him and shook his head. "You're telling me Katerina sold Lucy a curse that bound you to that vile witch?"

"Yes."

"And you're letting her stay at your house?" he asked incredulously.

Braxton sighed. "She promised to find a way to break the curse. That's the only reason I let her stay."

"And you believe her?" Dante looked like he was ready to murder someone.

"No, but I have to give it a chance." Braxton took Lily's hand in his and pulled her close to him.

Dante looked between the two of them and then nodded slowly. "I see."

"I thought you might," Braxton said.

Dante nodded. "I've got your back if you need anything. A buffer from spelled chicks, a day off to spend with your girl, a hand sending your mother the hell out of town. Name it. I'm there."

Braxton grinned at him. "Thanks, man."

Dante nodded and then looked at Lily. "Take care of him."

"I plan to." She smiled up at Braxton. Then as Dante headed to the other side of the store, she frowned. "You never told Dante about the curse?"

He shook his head. "I don't like talking about it. It's awful to tell people your own mother is a psycho. Not that Dante didn't already know she was a grifter and a cheat. But this is another level. The only people who knew were the few women I dated, you, and now Dante."

"What? Niko doesn't know either?" she asked, sounding shocked.

"Nope." Braxton shook his head.

Lily frowned, looking troubled.

"Don't worry, I'll tell him eventually," Braxton said. "It just hasn't come up." He reached down and pulled her to him. As her arms wrapped around him, Braxton's heart warmed, and he decided he never wanted to let go.

But when they heard the bell on the door chime a second later, he pulled back and smiled at Niko as he walked in.

Niko waved at Brax and then cleared his throat. "Hello, Lily, nice to see you again."

Lily glanced at him, her lips curving into a small frown. "Niko."

"I heard a rumor today that you're a Befana witch," Niko said.

"Guilty," she said, her voice flat. "My grandmother is Bethany Befana."

He gave her an approving nod. "That's a powerful line."

"Yeah, but it's not something we tend to brag about." Lily looked him up and down with suspicion. "Why do you care?"

The tension streaming off Lily was palpable, and Braxton wondered what had happened to make Lily so wary of his friend. Did it have something to do with him hooking up with her sister? Or maybe she was still troubled by Prim's intuitive feeling that something was off with Niko. Lily could be protective. He knew that firsthand.

"I don't. Just thought it was interesting." He turned to Braxton. "Do you have a schedule for those kayak tours that are booked? I want to put them on my calendar so I make sure and show up on the right days."

"Kayak tours?" Lily asked.

"Niko is taking them over while he's here to help us out," Braxton said.

"Really?" Lily asked, looking even more surly than she

had when Niko first walked in. "So all three of you are working here now?"

"For the time being," Niko said. "Until I figure out my next move."

"Niko's always the unpredictable one," Dante said, coming up behind Niko and placing both hands on his shoulders, shaking him slightly until Niko twisted and put him in a headlock. The two continued to wrestle just like they had as kids until Niko let Dante go, and all three of them laughed.

"Boys," Lily muttered.

Niko's phone buzzed, and when he glanced at it, he turned back to Braxton and said, "I have to take this. It's important. Can we go over the schedule later today?"

"Sure," Braxton said with a nod.

As Niko left the store, Braxton wondered what the important phone call was about. He was happy to see his friend, but he had to admit that despite the playful wrestling, the guy who had suddenly arrived in Befana Bay was quite a bit different from the one he knew in high school. But that was to be expected. They'd all grown up in the past fifteen years. But Niko seemed to have an air of mystery about him that was starting to make Braxton a little uneasy, and he didn't know why.

Lily slipped her hand into Braxton's and said, "Do you have a minute? Are you busy?"

"No, it's been pretty quiet. Let's—"

The bell chimed again, and this time his mother walked into the store. Her bright red hair was windblown, and she looked a little frantic as she glanced around the store. When she spotted Braxton, she rushed over to him. "There you are."

"Where else would I be?" he asked, annoyed that she'd come to the store in the middle of the day. It was hard enough knowing that she was living in his garage apartment. Having her intrude on his daily life was a step too far, especially after he'd expressly warned her she wasn't welcome in the store. He opened his mouth to say as much, but then his mother spotted Lily.

"Who's that?" Katerina pointed at Lily, and her lips twisted into a scowl.

"This is Lily Easton," he said and then bent down to whisper to Lily, "This is my mom, Katerina."

"You know you can't date anyone, Braxton," Katerina admonished as she stared at their entwined hands.

"That's not up for discussion," he said flatly. "Why don't you just tell me why you're here? Have you found Lucy yet?"

Katerina pulled her glare from Lily and suddenly looked contrite. "No, but I wanted you to know I set up a meeting with the town coven for tomorrow morning to ask them for their help."

"What time?" Lily demanded.

"I don't think that's any of your concern." Katerina sniffed, dismissing her.

Lily let out a humorless laugh. "Oh, it's my business, all right, since I'm the one dating your son. I'll be at that coven meeting whether you like it or not."

His mother looked horrified by Lily's declaration. "If you know what's good for you, you'll stay away from that meeting. It's far too dangerous for a young witch like you."

Braxton glared at his mother, wishing he could physically throw her from his shop. If it hadn't been for the curse still being active, he might have.

"I don't think I'm going to take advice from a grifter witch, but thanks anyway," Lily spat out.

Braxton squeezed her hand, showing silent support. It felt good having someone by his side, standing up to his mother.

Lily returned his squeeze and pressed up on her tiptoes to kiss him on his cheek. "I have to go, but I'll call you later. We'll talk then."

When Lily dropped his hand, he ached to pull her back to him. But he kept his hands to himself as he watched her go.

The moment she was gone, Dante walked back over and let out a low whistle. "You've got a firecracker on your hands, Brax. I bet she's a handful."

Braxton glared at his friend. "That's enough."

"You're playing with fire, Braxton," his mother warned. "Something awful is going to happen if you keep this up."

"And who's fault is that?" Dante said accusingly.

"Stay out of this. It doesn't concern you." Katerina seethed as she glared at Brax's friend.

"It sure the hell does when you're the reason my best friend is cursed," Dante shot back.

Brax gave his friend a nod of solidarity. "Thanks, Dante, but I've got it from here."

Dante returned his nod and then scowled at Katerina as he retreated, giving Braxton and his mother space.

Braxton gave his mother a cold hard stare. "I'm tired of

hearing what you think I can and can't do. No one asked for your opinion. So keep it to yourself. Got it?"

Katerina narrowed her eyes at him and looked like she wanted to spit nails. Braxton was braced for a diatribe, but when she spoke, she said, "I have to go. I'll let you know how the meeting goes tomorrow."

"You do that."

Katerina stalked out of the store, and as she trudged down the sidewalk, he said a silent prayer for patience.

CHAPTER 17

LILY'S FINGERS flew over the keyboard of her computer as she searched the county website for homes that were scheduled to be auctioned. She took a sip of her tea as she scrolled and then sat up when she spotted the small blue home in Hansville.

"I'll be damned," she muttered to herself. "It *is* up for auction." She had to admit that Niko was likely telling the truth, and him being there probably didn't have anything to do with looking for Lucy. Especially since she now knew that Braxton had never told him about the curse. Houses that were up for auction often weren't open for public viewing, so anyone interested in bidding would have to check it out from the outside. She sat back in her chair, pulled out her phone, and called Braxton.

His phone rang twice before it went straight to voice mail. She didn't want to have a one-sided conversation, so she ended the call and texted him, asking him to call when he had a chance. She still needed to tell him that she'd found Lucy's last known address and that his ex was most likely in the area.

A text came back almost immediately. He was dealing with a leaky pipe at his house and would call when he could.

Lily sighed. It was always something. She glanced at the clock and yawned. It had been a long day, her eyes were starting to water, and she had to be up early to work on the rest of the details for the Midsummer Festival. They had gotten almost everything done except for finalizing the website. Lily had volunteered to handle all the updates since Braxton wasn't as computer savvy as she was. And since the festival was coming up fast, she wanted to get it done before eleven o'clock, when she had to be at her grandmother's for the coven meeting. There was no way Lily was going to miss that.

Katerina Kirkwood would just have to live with it.

Lily sent one last message to Braxton, letting him know she was headed to bed and that she'd talk to him tomorrow. When her weary body finally hit the sheets, she fell into a deep sleep within seconds.

LILY HELD BACK a grimace when she glanced out the window and spotted Katerina Kirkwood climbing the stairs to her grandmother's porch. It was five minutes after eleven, and the coven meeting had just started. Her grandmother and the other five witches who were present were not impressed.

"Looks like our guest has finally arrived," Bethany said with an air of irritation.

"I'll let her in," Lily said, jumping to her feet and heading for the foyer. She yanked the front door open and found Katerina with her fist up, clearly getting ready to knock. "You're late."

"I thought the meeting started at 11:00?" she said, sounding confused.

"It did." Lily held the door open and ushered the woman in. They were silent as they made their way into the parlor, where the meeting was being held.

"This is Katerina Kirkwood," Lily said. "Katerina, this is my grandmother, Bethany Befana, and the rest of the Befana Bay coven. I've already filled them in on your history, so don't bother trying to sugarcoat it."

Katerina sent Lily a death glare so vile that if a curse had been attached to it, Lily was certain her heart would've already stopped.

"Take a seat Katerina," Bethany said. "Lily tells us you're trying to reverse a curse you sold to a young woman some years back."

"Yes," Katerina said, sitting with her hands in her lap. "The curse bound my son to her, and now if he has a relationship with anyone other than her, the relationship is doomed."

"Destruction of the Heart Curse," Serena, the witch sitting to the right of Bethany, said. Her tone was dripping with judgment.

Katerina gave a tiny nod. "Yes. That's the one."

"You do realize that's illegal, right?" Serena asked.

"I don't cast those kinds of curses anymore," Katerina said, her eyes full of apprehension. "I admit I made mistakes." She let out a nervous laugh. "Doesn't everyone at some point in their lives?"

"Not those kinds of mistakes," a darked-haired witch named Jacinda said. She was wearing a white linen suit that made her look like she should be on a southern porch sipping mint juleps.

The other remaining witches all nodded, supporting Jacinda's statement.

"Well, aren't we judgmental," Katerina muttered to herself.

Bethany stood up and cleared her throat. "From everything I've heard, you're the type of witch who belongs behind bars. I'd be careful about what you say while in this room, Katerina. If the witches of Befana Bay are judging you, it appears there is good reason. You have been allowed an audience here for one reason and one reason only. Braxton is a valued member of this community. If there is something we can do to help him, we will. But understand that helping *you* is not something any of us are eager to do. Now, please state your case for what it is you think we can do to help Braxton."

Katerina's face flushed a deep red as she clenched her fists in her lap. Lily couldn't help the satisfaction that washed over her, knowing that Katerina was humiliated. The woman deserved no less after everything she'd put Braxton through.

"I would like to reverse the curse that was cast on Braxton." Katerina swallowed hard and continued. "Since I made it, all we need is a coven powerful enough to break it. I was hoping that, for Braxton's sake, you all would be willing to help do that as soon as possible."

Serena scoffed. "You want us to do a curse reversal without the witch who cast it?"

"We don't have a choice," Katerina said meekly. "I've been looking for Lucy for a number of years now but haven't been able to find her. You don't know how much it's eaten away at me that I'm the one responsible for what happened to my son. I just don't think I can go on living like this. We have to find a way to break the curse."

Unease bubbled in Lily's gut, and she knew in that moment that Katerina wasn't being entirely truthful. There was something about her story that was off. She wasn't here because of guilt over what she'd done to her son. There was another reason. "You're lying," Lily blurted. "Tell them why you're really here."

Serena glanced at Lily and then back at Katerina, her voice eerily calm when she said, "Your lies are not permitted here."

"But I'm not lying!" Katerina got to her feet and placed her hands on her hips as she stared down at Lily. "Stay out of this. You don't know anything about me or my son."

Bethany reached out and placed her hand on Katerina's shoulder, giving Braxton's mother a slight shove and forcing her to sit again. "You will remain respectful to all the witches here, or you can leave. Your choice."

Katerina sucked in her cheeks, looking like she'd just sucked on a lemon.

Lily was torn between laughing and throwing her out.

Katerina might have been asking the coven to help break Braxton's curse, but she wasn't there out of the goodness of her heart. Lily was certain of it. Breaking the curse had to benefit Katerina in some way. Lily just didn't know how. Still, if it freed Braxton, Lily didn't really care what the reason was. She just wanted the man she was falling in love with to finally be free.

"You say you've been looking for the woman who cast the curse," Bethany said. "What steps did you take to find her?"

"Steps?" Katerina asked, her voice hesitant.

"Yes, steps." Bethany was impatient now. "What have you done to find her?"

"Um, well, I've done multiple internet searches and have asked about her among the people I've… uh, done business with. Lucy's a ghost. There's not one trace of her on social media."

Lily gave Katerina a flat stare. For a grifter and a scammer, her effort was sorely lacking.

"You didn't hire a private investigator?" Serena asked, sounding just as irritated as Bethany.

"I, um, don't have the resources for that," Katerina stammered.

"The answer is no," Serena said.

"But—" Katerina started.

"It would take all of us to be in agreement," Bethany said, cutting her off. "If one is out, then we all are. Frankly, I'm in agreement with Serena. There is more to be done to find this Lucy woman. It's much too risky to try to break the spell without the person who is bound to Braxton." Bethany put an arm around her granddaughter. "I am not willing to put anyone else at risk because of your reckless behavior. When you've found Lucy, then come talk to us. Until then, you're not welcome in this house."

Katerina sat in her chair, motionless, her mouth hanging open.

"That means you're dismissed," Serena said. She gestured to Lily. "Can you see Ms. Kirkwood out, please?"

"Of course." Lily took Katerina by her arm and tugged for her to move. When she didn't, Lily hauled her up and said, "Go."

The movement seemed to prod Katerina out of her shocked stupor. She planted her feet and cried, "You can't do this! Do you understand what this means? Time is running out! If this doesn't happen soon, it won't happen at all. You have to help me."

"We don't *have* to do anything, Ms. Kirkwood," Bethany said, her tone full of ice. "Now please go. I'm sure you'd rather leave under your own power than have me and the rest of the coven escort you out."

"You're the reason I always stayed away from covens," Katerina called over her shoulder as she stomped toward the foyer. "So high and mighty and full of yourselves."

"I'd stop your ranting if I were you," Lily said as she followed the woman. "Once they lose their patience, it won't be pleasant."

"Pleasant. As if there was anything tolerable about that meeting. They get off on making people like me feel small. Well, forget it. I don't need their help. I'll figure out how to break the curse myself."

Lily opened the door for her. "I hope you do," Lily said honestly, even though she knew it would be impossible unless she found Lucy. "Braxton deserves better."

Katerina didn't say another word as she left the big Victorian house and disappeared around the corner.

Lily closed the door softly and went back into the coven meeting.

"I'm sorry, Lily," her grandmother said. "I know you were hoping for a better outcome."

"I was," Lily said. "But all hope isn't lost. Braxton's mom might not have the resources for a private investigator, but I do. When I find Lucy, I'll let you know."

"You do that, dear." Bethany gave her a hug and then sat back in her seat and clasped her hands together. "Now, let's get on with the important stuff. Who's in charge of the magical beautification of the grounds in front of the post office?"

CHAPTER 18

FEELING out of sorts and more than a little disappointed by the coven's decision to ignore Katerina's request, Lily climbed into her car and just started driving. She understood the reasoning behind refusing to break the curse, and if she'd been in their shoes, she was certain she'd have made the same decision. It was dangerous. There was no doubt about that. It was just that she was the one who was at risk and felt it should be her decision.

If they'd left it up to her, would she have said yes to trying it before they found Lucy?

Probably not. Especially not when she had a lead on the woman.

There was nothing to do but find Lucy.

Before Lily even realized what she was doing, she turned around and pointed her car in the direction of Hansville. Maybe this time she'd get lucky and find the one woman who could end all this turmoil.

Even though the town was fairly close, Lily felt like she'd never get there. By the time she made the turn onto Lucy's street, she was vibrating with anticipation.

The house appeared to be just as deserted as the day before. She cursed under her breath and drove down the block, intending to park in the same spot she and Prim had used.

But a black Ford Bronco with a rental tag was already parked in her spot.

She didn't even bother trying to hide from him. Lily quickly parked her car and stalked over to the Bronco, knocking rapidly on the black tinted window. "Niko, I know that's you in there. Open up!"

The window lowered, and the man in question said, "Lily? What are you doing here?"

"What am I doing here? What are *you* doing here?"

"This house is scheduled to go to auction. I was hoping that someone would show up to let me see the inside," he said with such ease that she almost believed him.

But not quite.

"That's a lie," she said, placing her hands on her hips and glaring at him. "What are you really doing here?"

He shrugged and gave her an easy smile. "Looking out for a friend."

"So you *do* know about—" She stopped abruptly, not wanting to spill Braxton's secret if Niko didn't already know.

His grinned widened. "Know about what?"

"I hate you," she said in frustration.

"I can tell." When she didn't respond, his smiled fell and he relented. "I told you; I'm here looking out for a friend."

"Which friend?" she asked, studying him carefully.

"Which one do you think? Braxton, of course."

"Do you know who lives here?" Lily didn't want to mention Lucy until he did.

"Yes. Do you?"

"Yes."

"Then we're both here for the same reason, aren't we?" he said evenly.

Lily blew out a frustrated breath. "Just tell me how you know. Because Braxton told me that he didn't even confide in his friends."

"How I know isn't important," Niko said. "All that matters now is finding Lucy and helping Braxton out of this mess. Right?"

"Sure," Lily agreed.

"Then can we work together?" he asked, assessing her.

"Hell, no. How do I know you're not a lying creep?" Lily still didn't trust him. She couldn't get a read on his vibe, and that made her uneasy. The fact that he knew about the curse without Braxton telling him also set off warning bells. Dante hadn't even known. And now Niko was staking out Lucy's house without even telling Braxton about it? She just didn't trust him.

I'm the lying creep?" he asked with an amused laugh. "That's rich. Does Brax know *you're* here?"

"No. I just came today on a whim. I didn't have a chance to tell him yesterday. First, you were there, and I wanted to talk to him alone. And then his mom showed up, and I certainly wasn't going to talk about this with her around."

"That was smart at least." He waved a hand. "Get in."

"No way." She placed her hands on her hips. "You think I'm crazy enough to get into a car with someone who's been lying to everyone?"

"Would you rather be out there if Lucy comes home?" he asked, ignoring her accusation.

Crap. He had a point. "How do I know you're not going to take me to some undisclosed place and lock me in a dungeon?"

Niko actually laughed. "I guess that's a risk you'll just have to take."

Lily hated that she couldn't get a solid read on the man. Usually she could just sense a person's aura. But his was just sort of blank, like it was being shrouded by magic. She noted that the Bronco wasn't running and decided, if he did try to take off, she'd have enough time to jump out before she was kidnapped. With a sigh, she walked around to the passenger side and got in.

"Now," she said, "how did you know this is Lucy's place?"

"Probably the same way you did," he said.

"I had a friend run a trace on her, and this address popped up," Lily said, not seeing any reason to keep it a secret.

"That's impressive." He gave her an approving nod. "It wasn't easy to find."

"Ressa's the best."

He gave her a side-eye glance. "Do you often find yourself needing a private investigator?"

"Yes." She didn't offer an explanation. So far she was the only one explaining herself. "Do you?"

"They come in handy sometimes." His gaze locked on a blue Toyota as it rolled down the street. When it passed Lucy's house and kept going, he turned his attention back to Lily. "What exactly does a woman like you from a small town need a PI for?"

"It's a town of witches. Sometimes things go haywire." She smirked. When he just stared at her, she rolled her eyes and said, "We get a lot of celebrities in town. We need background checks for those who work with them."

"I see. Makes sense."

"Now it's your turn. Why do you need PIs?" she demanded.

"That's not important. I'm just here looking after Braxton. He doesn't need any more trouble in his life, and if I can help him with that, I will. My only question is, are you helping him, or are you in cahoots with Lucy?"

Lily reared back as if she'd been slapped. "In cahoots with his crazy, curse-wielding ex? How dare you? I'm here because I care about Braxton and want to break the curse so he can move on in peace."

Niko took a long moment to study her and then nodded. "Yeah, I think you mean that."

"I don't need your approval."

"You're right. You don't." He stared her in the eye and said, "But fair warning; I'm not who you think I am, and I'll just caution you that you better be telling the truth. Otherwise, you'll have to answer to me."

"Are you threatening me?" she asked through clenched teeth.

"Just making conversation."

Lily was so angry she could have spit. "I don't like you. I know Brax thinks you're a friend, but I don't trust you. Stay away from both of us and my sister." Before he could answer, she climbed out of his Bronco and ran for her car.

Then she took one last look at the deserted blue house before speeding off to find Braxton.

LILY WAS STILL out of sorts when she walked into The Enchanted Outdoors. "Dante?" she called when she spotted him stocking one of the shelves.

He jerked his head up. "Lily. What can I do for you?"

"Where's Brax?"

"In the back."

"Thanks," she said and took off through the door to the stock room as if she owned the place.

Braxton was just putting the phone down when he spotted her and stood. "Lily, what—"

"I need to tell you something," she blurted.

"Okay." He pulled out a chair for her and sat back down. "What is it? Did something happen? Nothing blew up, did it?"

"No, nothing like that. At least not yet." She took a moment to collect herself before she blurted, "I found Lucy."

He blinked, clearly shocked into silence. When he finally spoke, he repeated, "You found Lucy?"

"Yes. I asked our PI to run a background check and a trace on her. One of her aliases signed a lease for a house in Hansville two months ago."

Braxton's face drained of color. "She's here in Washington?"

"I think so. I went to her house and—"

He stood abruptly. "You went to her house?"

"Yes. I wanted to see if it was her first."

"And?" he asked.

"I can't be sure. No one was there both times I went over, but—"

"Wait, both times? How long have you known?" He was frowning, looking upset.

"Since yesterday morning. Prim went with me, and then I was going to tell you yesterday, but Niko... And then your mom was there. I just wanted to talk to you alone, but you were fixing your plumbing, and it's just been one thing after another. I'm here now."

He sat back down and moved his chair closer, taking her hands in his. "I think you need to start at the beginning."

"Right." She explained her conversation with Ressa and then her impromptu trip with Prim, only to be foiled by Niko. And then that she discovered that the house really was scheduled to go up for auction.

"Okay, so he's possibly looking to buy a place. That makes sense. He's always been a guy who likes a bargain," Braxton reasoned. "Strange coincidence though."

She snorted. "Yes, especially since I found him there

again today, and he admitted that he knew Lucy had rented the house."

"What?" Braxton's entire body tensed. "He knows about the curse? How?"

"I have no idea. He didn't say. He just told me he's looking out for his friend and..." She shrugged. "He wouldn't tell me much. Honestly, I think he suspected me of somehow partnering with Lucy. As cagey as he was, he was very protective of you," she admitted.

The tension drained from Brax's body. "He's always been protective. I think you two have that in common," he said with a soft smile.

"He was not nice to me, Brax." She knew she sounded petulant, but she had to tell him everything. "I don't know why he didn't just tell you he knows about the curse and that he was looking for Lucy."

"You didn't tell me you'd found her or that you went to her house," he said, though his tone was kind.

"That's different. I told you I was looking for her so I could find a way to break the curse. It's not like I was trying to keep anything from you. I was planning on telling you."

"I believe you. I still don't think there's any reason to suspect that Niko's motivations are any different. He's here with a lot of time on his hands. I don't know how he found out, and I wish he'd talked to me about it, but I bet he wanted to see if he could find anything first. I don't know. But one thing I do know for sure is that he's an honorable guy."

Lily sat back in her chair. "Okay, but you should know I

got a weird feeling from him, and my intuition is almost always right."

"I'll talk to him," he promised. Then he looked at the clock. It was just past one. "How about we get out of here for a while? Just you and me. Maybe take a hike like we talked about before?"

"I'd love that. But I need to stop at home to change first."

"We'll stop there first." He led her out into the store and told Dante he was taking off for the day.

Dante waved. "See you later."

When Braxton pulled up to Lily's house, he reached behind the seat and produced a pair of hiking shoes. "I'll get these on while you're changing."

"Okay. I'll be right out." Lily rushed into the house, got herself ready for the hike, and grabbed two water bottles on the way out, feeling better than she had in days. The idea of spending a little time away from their problems felt like heaven. She was still upset about what went down with Niko, but Braxton seemed to be taking it in stride, so she was determined to try and do the same.

When she hopped back into the truck, she stuck the water bottle in the cup holders. "I figured we could use these."

"Good thinking," Braxton said and took off for the trailhead.

CHAPTER 19

BRAXTON PULLED up to Lily's house and killed the engine. Their afternoon of hiking had done wonders to clear his mind. After learning that Lucy was in Washington and that Niko somehow knew about the curse and was apparently trying to find Lucy, too, he'd needed something to distract himself. Otherwise, he'd have lost it. The very Idea that Lucy had followed him to Washington made him want to punch a wall. What awful, destructive thing was she up to now? He really didn't want to know. All he cared about was breaking the curse, and if she was nearby, that meant she'd be easier to find.

Soon enough he'd talk to Niko and then confront his mother. He didn't believe for a second that she didn't know Lucy was nearby. It was likely the reason she was in Washington at all. She either wanted Lucy back as a partner, or she wanted to destroy her for leaving in the first place.

He'd known all along that his mother probably wouldn't hold up her end of the deal. But he'd had to try.

"Do you want to come in? I could make dinner," Lily said.

He reached over and cupped her cheek. "There's nothing I'd like more, but I really need to take care of a few things."

Lily chewed on her bottom lip. "Do those things include talking to Niko and seeing what your mom knows about Lucy?"

"You read my mind," he said with a wry smile.

"Honestly, I was surprised you didn't do that right after our talk earlier today." Lily placed her hand over his and squeezed.

"I needed a bit of time to let it sink in. Thank you for going on the hike with me. It was exactly what I needed."

"Any time." Lily leaned into his touch and closed her eyes for a brief second.

She looked so lovely that it made Braxton's heart squeeze. He leaned in and brushed his lips over hers. She tasted like sunshine and strawberries, and he wanted more. When he deepened the kiss, she wrapped her arms around him and let out a soft moan.

It made him want to carry her into her house and taste every inch of her skin. His body was alive with need, desperate for a night alone with her. But this time he wouldn't hold back. He wanted her, wanted to make her his in every sense of the word.

"Brax," she murmured breathlessly. "I want you."

He groaned and forced himself to retreat. Her eyes were glazed with lust, and her lips were red and kiss-swollen. It was nearly enough to make him stay. "I think it's obvious I want you, too." His voice was gruff and full of need. "But not tonight. Not until—"

"The curse is broken," she finished with a sigh, looking disappointed.

He hated himself. "I'm sorry. I just don't want that hanging between us when I finally make love to you."

She gave him a weak smile. "How can I argue with that?"

Braxton leaned in and kissed her again. They stayed wrapped in each other's arms for what seemed like forever, until Lily was the one to pull back. She ran her thumb over his jawline and said, "I have to go in now. But promise me we'll find a way to break this curse soon, otherwise, I think we're both going to combust sooner rather than later."

"It's a promise." He didn't know how, but he'd find a way.

She jumped out of his truck and ran up to her house. Once she was inside, Braxton headed home, dread already coiling in his gut as he told his phone to call Niko.

The phone rang five times before his friend's voice mail clicked on.

"Niko, it's Brax. Call me as soon as you get this. It's important."

After he parked in his long driveway, he didn't bother going into his house. He headed straight for the garage apartment, but even as he climbed the stairs, he had a sinking suspicion that his mother wasn't there. The lights weren't on, and none of the windows were open. It was one of her things. She always needed a window open. She said she felt caged in without it.

He knocked anyway, and when she didn't answer, he let

himself in. The bed was unmade and there were dishes piled high in the sink. He made a noise of disgust and headed back down the stairs to his house.

After tossing his keys in the bowl next to the door, he called out, "Dante?"

No answer.

Brax was striking out all over, and he instantly regretted leaving Lily. He could've been wrapped in her arms instead of pacing his living room. The very thought of her sent a shot of lust through him.

"Hello, Brax," a soft, very unwelcome voice said from behind him.

He turned and clutched at the stairway banister. "Lucy. Long time no see."

"As soon as I heard you were here in Washington, I knew I had to come see you." The petite woman had died her brown hair platinum blond, and instead of being dressed in an oversized boho-style dress like she'd worn when they were together, she was dressed in jeans and some sort of low-cut wraparound shirt that showed off her ample cleavage. She'd topped the look off with six-inch stiletto heels.

"Why? Are you here to cast another curse? My mother is living in the garage apartment. I'm sure she'd be happy to sell you another one, though she swears she's given up the life. But I'm pretty sure neither one of us would believe her."

"Brax, come on now." She made a pouty face. "That's not why I'm here, and you know it."

"You think so? Because I really have no clue. My best

guess is that you and my mother have teamed up to find a way to ruin my life again."

She sighed. "I can see you're still angry. Fine, I'll get right to the point. The reason I'm here is to offer you a deal."

He scoffed. "You want me to make a deal with you? You're out of your mind."

"Maybe. But what if I offered to break the curse? Then you could go off and make babies with that mousey blonde you seem to like so much."

Unadulterated rage surged through his veins. "You've been watching me and Lily?"

She smirked. "You didn't think I'd come here without doing my research, did you?"

He wanted to strangle her. "There aren't going to be any deals, Lucy. You're going to break this curse and then leave me, Lily, and the rest of this town the hell alone. Got it?"

"Sure. But you're going to do something for me first." She gave him a wide smile that didn't reach her eyes.

"Why would I do anything for you?" He glared at her, wondering what he ever saw in the woman standing before him.

"Because if you don't, not only are you going to be saddled with this curse forever, but your mom, your girlfriend, and her entire family are all going to end up magical eunuchs."

He stared at her, processing what she was saying. "That's impossible," he finally said. There was no way she had that much power. His mother, sure… Maybe Lucy could strip Katerina of her power. But the Befana witches? He started to laugh. "You've taken one too many potions. I think it's rotted your brain."

Lucy narrowed her eyes at him, hatred streaming off her in waves. "You have no idea the power I've acquired over the years, Braxton Kirkwood. The only thing that's holding me back now is you and that nosy friend of yours you sicced on me."

"What are you talking about? I didn't sic anyone on you." Was she crazy? All he'd ever tried to do was find her to break the curse and move on with his life.

"Pay attention, Braxton. I'm talking about the one who has been hounding me for the past three years. Your buddy at the Magical Task Force. He's getting on my last nerve, and *you're* going to get him off my ass. In return I'll break the curse, and we can live the rest of our lives pretending we never met."

"I have no idea what you're talking about," Braxton said, staring at her in complete confusion. "I don't know anyone in the Magical Task Force."

"Don't lie to me, Braxton. It won't end well for you," she said in a sinister tone.

That pissed him off. "If anyone is a liar, it's you, Lucy Lansing. I have no idea what you're ranting about. Your paranoia has gotten the better of you. I don't know what you *think* you know, but it's all bullshit. Now break this curse and leave me alone, or I *will* find a way to turn you into the Magical Task Force again."

"You haven't changed," she said, shaking her head. "Still the naïve dreamer I fell in love with all those years ago." There was a nostalgia in her tone now that made Braxton's skin crawl. "Maybe I was wrong," she continued, smiling sweetly at him. "Maybe I don't want to sever the connection."

"Lucy," he warned, moving toward her. "Don't do this. You haven't missed me all these years, otherwise you'd have come back sooner. Can't we just end this and move on?"

"I'll never be able to move on. Not now. Not when they're going to haul me off to prison for crimes *your* mother forced me to commit," she spat out. "It's *your* fault she came into my life. Why should you lead a happy life while I spend mine on the run? No, that's not going to happen. I think it's time you came home to me, where you can pay for the sins of your mother."

"Lucy, I—"

A bolt of magic hit him right in the chest, sending Braxton to the floor. The last thing he saw was Lucy peering over him, shaking her head as his world turned black.

CHAPTER 20

LILY FLOATED INTO HER HOUSE, feeling like she was living in a dream. She'd desperately wanted Braxton to come inside after their hike, but she understood why he hadn't. There was still this curse between them, and when they finally committed themselves to each other, he wanted them to be free to love without any other energy tainting them.

He was right.

Plus, they still didn't know if the curse would get worse if they got closer.

She headed first for a shower and then grabbed something to eat. After the sun went down, she made a cup of tea and headed out onto her back porch to take in the stars and enjoy the cool summer night air. It was just one of those nights when the outdoors called to her. She supposed it was from being in the woods earlier in the day with Braxton. She didn't want to let go of that feeling.

She was laying in her hammock, staring at the trees

when she spotted a flash of yellow that looked like eyes staring back at her. She sat up and scanned again. After a moment, a pure white wolf walked out of the trees and stared right at her, its golden eyes flashing to blue.

Lily's heart sped up, and her breath caught as recognition dawned. A white wolf with eyes that changed to blue. There was no question the wolf was the exact same one they'd spotted on Westerly Island just days before.

Wolves were already extremely rare in their neck of the woods. The chances of there being two that were identical was nonexistent.

"Hey, handsome," she said in a quiet voice. "How did you get over here from the island?"

The wolf stood still, staring at her.

"Don't tell me you snuck on the ferry," she mused. "Clever, aren't you?"

There was a loud pounding at her front door, grabbing her attention. When she looked back for the wolf, he was gone. Disappointment washed over her, and she let out a grunt of irritation as she went inside to see what all the commotion was about.

"Hold on," she cried. "I'm coming. Geeze. You don't need to break the door down." She yanked the door open and found Niko standing on her porch, his expression dire. "What the hell's going on? You look like someone stole your puppy."

"Is Brax here?" Niko demanded.

"No. Isn't he at home?" she asked, suddenly concerned.

He shook his head. "His truck is there. So are his keys and wallet. But he is not."

Lily's head swam, and she swayed on her feet but grabbed the door to steady herself. "Maybe he went for a walk?"

"Is that something he does regularly?" he asked.

"No. I don't know. He probably didn't take a walk," Lily said. "We went on a hike today, so I don't know why he'd go home and head back out. I'm just trying to figure out what might have happened."

Niko brushed past her and walked into her house, not waiting for an invitation. He turned to face her. "When was the last time you saw him?"

Lily pressed her hand to her throat as she tried to think back to what time Braxton dropped her off. "I don't know. Maybe around six o'clock? We went on our hike and then he brought me back here. I thought he was heading home."

Niko nodded. "His truck is there, so that's a pretty good assumption."

"Have you talked to Dante? Maybe he's with him."

"Dante is at the house now. He's the one who called me when he couldn't find Brax. When Dante called Braxton, he heard his phone ring and found it under the armchair, the face shattered. The door wasn't locked either. There's no hard evidence of foul play, but Braxton has just vanished, and I have reason to believe that someone may have taken him."

Ice ran through Lily's veins. "Where is Katerina?"

He pressed his lips into a tight line and shook his head. "No one knows."

"Do you think she's the one who took him?"

"No. She's not strong enough," he said.

"Do you think Lucy showed up and they got into it?" Lily couldn't think of anyone else. "Or maybe another one of my readers got to him?" She sank down into a chair, holding her head in her hands. If someone had gone psycho on him, it would be all her fault. She was the one who kept pushing for the relationship. He'd told her that it was too dangerous, but she hadn't listened.

"We don't know anything yet," Niko said, his voice suddenly soothing. He reached down and squeezed her shoulder.

Lily glared up at him. "Stop being nice to me. You're making it worse."

His eyes were full of sympathy as he pulled his hand away. "I'm going to keep looking for Braxton. Call me if you see or hear from him, okay?"

"I will if you will." She stared up into his dark eyes. "Promise me you'll call as soon as you know anything."

"Either Dante or I will," he said and then left her alone, her thoughts reeling.

Lily racked her brain, trying to remember if any "Ask Endora" column she'd written joked about abducting someone instead of just talking out their issues. She'd certainly thought about writing such a scenario before but was pretty sure she'd stopped herself. It was too on the nose. Too predictable. Not to mention vile. She tried not to go *too* over the top with her advice. It was supposed to be funny, not tragic.

Either way, if anyone was to blame, Lily was certain it was her. They had spent the afternoon together on a hike that most normal people would call a date. Especially since they'd made out in his truck afterward. And made promises to each other once the curse was broken. If anything would kick the curse into high gear, it was that.

Hating herself for not listening to Braxton, Lily shoved her shoes on and took off out of her house, running full speed to her grandmother's. She was out of breath and didn't even bother knocking. She just barreled in and called, "Gran!"

There were footsteps at the top of the stairs, followed by Bethany calling, "Lily, is that you?"

"Yes, it's me. I need your help."

Bethany appeared on the stairs, wearing a gorgeous green-velvet robe. Her hair was pulled up into a messy bun, and her face was stripped of makeup.

"Oh, no. I caught you as you were getting ready for bed," Lily said as guilt ate away at her conscience. But the truth was, it wouldn't have mattered if her grandmother was already sleeping. She'd still have come. This was too important.

"It's okay, dear." Bethany came downstairs and grabbed Lily's hands and asked, "What's happened?"

"It's Braxton. He's vanished, and no one knows where he is. I was the last one to see him and then… poof. Just gone. I'm afraid something terrible has happened to him. That the curse—" Her voice caught on a sob. "It's all my fault. Brax warned me, and I just thought… I don't know what I thought."

"Slow down." Bethany led her over to the couch and pulled her to sit down next to her. "What do you mean, he vanished?"

Lily explained how his truck was home and how they found his phone, but no Braxton. "I'm afraid that after we spent the afternoon together, maybe someone took some of my terrible advice and went over there, and things got out of hand or something."

"Or someone else came for him," Bethany said, frowning. "His mother does have quite the past. It's possible one of her acquaintances has a grievance and is using him to get to her."

"It's possible, I guess. But that's not making me feel any better." Her eyes stung with emotion as she stared at her grandmother. "We need to find him before something terrible happens."

"Yes, of course." Bethany stood. "Come with me. We'll do a finding spell."

Lily let out a breath and felt a tiny bit calmer as she followed her grandmother into her herb sanctuary.

"Do you have anything of Braxton's?" her grandmother asked.

"No." Lily wanted to kick herself. She should have known her grandmother would ask that. She chewed on her bottom lip, trying to think of something she might have of his back at her house. Her mind was blank. The truth was they hadn't spent that much time together. There hadn't been much opportunity to accumulate things at each other's homes.

"It's all right. Stand in the middle of the pentagram," Bethany said.

Once Lily did as she was told, Bethany handed her a pillar candle.

"Illuminate!" Bethany demanded. The candle flickered to life, and Bethany got down to business, chanting, "Goddess of life, here my call. Show us your son, Braxton Kirkwood, let your will be done." She repeated the words over and over and over again.

Lily waited for the rush of magic to wash over her, for the goddess to use her as a vessel to pinpoint Braxton's location.

But the magic barely brushed her skin, and the goddess never came.

Bethany lowered her outstretched hands and wiped at her own tear-filled eyes.

"Gran?" Lily asked tentatively. "What is it? What happened?"

"The locator spell didn't work, hon. I'm sorry."

"But it always works," Lily said, her voice trembling. "What does that mean?"

Bethany frowned, her expression looking pained. "It's one of two things, honey. Either someone has cloaked his energy or he's..."

"He's what?" Lily asked. "Gone? Dead? Is that what you're saying?"

Bethany nodded slowly.

"No!" Lily clutched her chest, her heart shredding to pieces. "He can't be gone. He was just with me this afternoon."

"Someone could be cloaking his magic," her grandmother reminded her.

"But you don't really believe that do you?" Lily challenged, taking her pain out on her grandmother.

"I don't know, honey. All I know is that I can't feel his energy. It won't come. So it's either being cloaked, or it doesn't exist."

"Call his spirit," Lily demanded.

Bethany nodded and stepped into the middle of the pentagram. Talking to spirits was one of Bethany's gifts. If Braxton had crossed over, she'd know. Her grandmother closed her eyes and started to center herself. After a few moments, she lifted her arms and called for Braxton Kirkwood.

Immediately, Bethany's eyes flew open, and she said, "He hasn't crossed over. Someone is cloaking his energy."

"Are you sure?" Lily asked, shocked by how fast the answer came.

"Positive. Half a dozen spirits descended on me to tell me that Braxton had not joined them."

Lily flung her arms around her grandmother and kissed her cheek. "Thank you. I love you. I need to go find Braxton."

"Yes, you do. Call if you hear anything or if you need the coven. We'll be ready for you." Bethany hugged and kissed her granddaughter and then sent her on her way.

CHAPTER 21

LILY PULLED into Braxton's driveway and parked behind his truck. She jumped out and scanned the inside of the vehicle, looking for anything that might be a clue as to where Braxton might be, but there was nothing except their two empty water bottles. She ignored the stab of pain that pierced her heart when she thought of how she'd just been with him a few hours ago.

"What are you doing here?" a shrill voice called.

Lily glanced over and spotted Katerina standing on the top of the stairs to the garage apartment. Her hands were balled into fists, and her eyes were shooting invisible daggers at Lily. "I'm looking for Braxton. What are you doing here?" Lily shot back.

"It's your fault he's gone. I told him that dating you was bad news." Katerina stomped down the stairs, still ranting. "I warned him that something terrible would happen. If you hadn't come along, my son would still be here."

"Me?" Lily scoffed. "You're the one who made that damned curse and gave it to Lucy. If anyone's at fault, it's you, you selfish piece of trash. What kind of mother does that to her only child? You have no business accusing me of anything, you lowlife scam artist."

"How dare you?" Katerina seethed as she straightened up, and fire flashed in her eyes.

Lily took a step back, not sure what to expect from Braxton's mother. She knew that Katerina had enough skill to make curses. It meant she had some formidable power. Though likely not as much as Lily.

Before Katerina could throw a spell at Lily, suddenly the older woman was out of breath and the fire had left her eyes. She grabbed onto the stair railing and slowly sat on the bottom step.

"You're not well," Lily said.

"What gave it away?" Katerina asked with an annoyed look. "The fact that I haven't already buried you with my magic or that I'm shaking and as pale as a ghost?"

"What's wrong with you?" Lily asked.

"None of your damned business."

"Her magic has been drained," Niko said from Braxton's front porch. "I imagine it's why she came crawling back to Braxton."

Lily glanced from Niko to Katerina and back to Niko. "I'm fairly certain that Braxton doesn't know that. How do you?"

"It's my job to know what people like Katerina are up to," he said and then walked back into the house.

"Is that true?" Lily asked Katerina. When the other

woman glanced away, she knew that Niko was telling the truth. "Did you ever have any intention of breaking Braxton's curse?"

"Yes," she snapped. "After he helped me get my powers back."

"Braxton was right; you really are a piece of work. Let me guess… Lucy stole your powers, and that's why you followed her here. In the meantime, you thought you could sponge off Brax and maybe get him to help you take her down, because after all, no one has a bigger grudge against her than he does."

Katerina just shook her head and slowly walked back up the stairs.

"Aren't you even going to try to help Brax?" Lily called after her.

"You, Niko, and Dante are here. You don't need my help." She walked into the apartment and slammed the door behind her.

Lily waited for a few moments to see if Katerina was going to come back out, but when she didn't, she headed for Braxton's house, determined to get answers from Niko. He'd opened a can of worms when he said it was his job to know what people like Katerina were up to. What did that mean, exactly?

But before she reached the front porch, she heard a rustling noise in the tree line to the left, and when she looked over, the large white wolf was standing there staring at her. She let out a small gasp of surprise. "You're back."

The wolf bowed its head and then swept it to the side, looking like he was gesturing for her to follow him. When he turned around and started trotting deeper into the trees, she didn't move until he looked back at her and let out a small *yip*.

Lily felt crazy for following a wolf into the woods, but she just knew she was supposed to. The wolf only went a few feet past the tree line before he stopped and pawed at the ground. Lily joined the wolf and when she looked down, she didn't see anything but darkness.

The wolf howled and pawed at the ground again.

"What is it?" she asked the wolf. "What am I supposed to be seeing?"

He pressed his nose to the ground, sniffed, and then darted forward, only to stop and look at her again with anticipation.

"You want me to follow you? I was already doing that."

The wolf pawed at the ground again, and Lily pulled out her phone to turn on the flashlight. When she did, she finally realized what he was showing her. There were footprints in the dirt, followed by what looked to be four-wheeler tracks.

"Did the person who attacked Brax go this way?" she asked the wolf.

He bobbed his head and whined, wanting to chase the tracks.

Lily's heart raced as she scrambled for what to do. If they were four-wheeler tracks, following on foot wouldn't do any good. Tracking them would take forever. But her car certainly wasn't going to be able to navigate the woods.

"Wait here. I'll be right back!" she called to the wolf as

she ran back toward Brax's house. She burst in through the front door. "Niko! Dante!"

Niko appeared from the kitchen. His phone was pressed to his ear. "Dante is out looking for Brax. What is it?"

"Tracks in the woods. We need to follow them. Does Brax have any four-wheelers?"

"I have to go. Call me if you find anything," Niko said into his phone. Then he ended the call and was already walking out the front door when he said, "Show me these tracks."

Lily ground her teeth together, frustrated that he was wasting time, but she quickly took him to where the wolf was still waiting. The wolf snarled at Niko, but when Lily said he was there to help, the wolf stopped, but he never took his eyes off the man.

"Dammit. She just drove him out of here," Niko said mostly to himself.

"She?" Lily asked. "You think this was Lucy?"

"Who else would it be?" He stood and started hurrying back toward the house. When they reached the garage, Niko wrapped his hand around the knob on the walk-in door and turned to Lily. "I've got it from here. Go back into the house and wait for Dante. I'll call when I've found him."

"Like hell!" Lily stood her ground. "I'm going to go after Braxton, and there's nothing you can say or do to stop me. I'll get a broom from my sister's store if that's what it takes. That wolf back there is showing me the way. Not you. *Me*. So either we go together, or I go by myself."

"A broom?" he asked, his lips twitching into a barely visible smile. "That would be something to see." He shook his head and led her into the garage. Moments later, they were in a four-seater ATV with Niko driving. He tossed her his phone. "Call Dante and tell him what we're doing."

Lily did as he asked, filling Dante in and asking him to let her grandmother know what was going on. If they ran into trouble, she wanted to know that the powerful witches of Befana Bay would know where to look for her.

"Wait!" Katerina jumped out in front of the side-by-side, waving her hands just before they moved into the woods. "Take me with you!"

"No," Lily said, shaking her head.

Niko stopped and let Katerina run over to them. "Why would we take you?"

"Because I can help. If Lucy did this, I know her. I understand what makes her tick. I'll be able to break the curse."

"You don't have any power," Niko said.

"I can take it back from her!" she cried.

Niko shook his head. "We don't need you in order to break the curse. You're not coming. Stay here. If you try to leave, you won't get far. My partner is watching you. Understand?"

"Partner?" Lily asked. What did that mean? Was that a romantic partner or a work partner?

Niko didn't answer, and Katerina started screaming at him, but he stepped on the gas, drowning her out, and shot into the woods where the wolf was still waiting.

The moment the wolf saw them, he took off through the trees.

Niko floored it, taking off into the woods.

"What did you mean by your partner?" she asked him, her voice raised over the engine noise.

"There's no partner. I was just trying to get her to stay put." He glanced at her quickly before turning his attention back to the woods.

"You haven't been running boat charters all these years, have you?" she asked.

Niko shook his head. "I've been tracking magical criminals."

"For the Magical Task Force?" she guessed.

He nodded.

"And you just happened to get assigned to a case that involved Braxton?"

"Not exactly." He gave her a wry smile.

His lack of detail in his answers was getting on her last nerve. "Spill it, Niko. Are you here on an official job, or are you off grid?"

He cast her a sidelong glance and said, "Both."

CHAPTER 22

BRAXTON WOKE with a jackhammer pounding on the inside of his skull. He groaned and curled up in a ball, his arms covering his head as if that would protect him from the massive headache that was trying to paralyze him.

"Oh, good. You're awake," Lucy said in a sweet voice. He felt the mattress dip beside him as she leaned over him and caressed his head. "I have your coffee ready. That and one of my potions will fix you right up."

He opened one eye and glared at her. "I wouldn't drink your potion if it was the last drop of liquid on earth."

Lucy jerked back, looking stricken. "What? Why? You've always taken them before. Is your stomach upset? I can make some toast."

Braxton stared at her, taking in her boho-chic outfit. She wore a flowing white blouse and matching skirt. She wore bangle bracelets on one arm and dangling sunflower earrings. Her face was freshly washed, and her hair was windblown as if she'd just come in from the beach. She didn't look anything like the woman who'd walked into his house the night before.

Had it been the night before? He wasn't sure. The weak morning sun was shining through the open window. It was barely dawn, and he assumed he'd only been out for the night, but with Lucy, one couldn't be too sure.

"Brax?" she asked, looking concerned. "I think you should take the potion. You'll feel better."

"I'd rather my head explode than take anything you made," he spat out.

"My, you've woken up on the wrong side of the bed." She gave him a flat stare and then retreated. "I think I'll check on you after you've had a chance to ease into the day."

If his head wasn't pounding, he thought he might have actually strangled her. Once the door slammed closed, he gingerly sat up in the queen-size bed and took stock of his physical situation. The pounding in his head had eased slightly, and his stomach was a little queasy, but otherwise, he thought he'd live.

That was unfortunate for Lucy, because once he got his hands on her, she was going to wish she'd killed him. He got to his feet, looking for a restroom. The en suite was just to his left. He disappeared into the bathroom, took care of business, and then splashed cold water on his face.

After sipping a bit of the water, he decided liquid was a good thing and went back to the bedside to inspect the coffee that Lucy had brought him. Holding the cup to his nose, he took a deep breath. All he could make out was the delicious scent of coffee. That didn't mean she hadn't hidden a potion in it though. Still, that headache was plaguing him, and he knew the caffeine would help. After taking the tiniest of sips, he decided it was safe.

Instantly, the coffee helped ease the ache in his head. He let out a sigh of relief and then took stock of his surroundings. He was obviously in the primary bedroom, and as he glanced around, a ball of unease filled his gut. He recognized this room. The bedspread. The drapes on the window. The sunset photography over the headboard.

The room was decorated exactly like their bedroom in the house they'd shared in Savannah when they were dating. Before she'd cursed him.

Cold sweat broke out over his body when he spotted a series of pictures hung on the opposite wall. They were of a small wedding party, and much to his dismay, Lucy was the bride and he was the groom.

Blinking rapidly to be sure he wasn't seeing things, he walked over to the series of four photos. Lucy was dressed in a simple white gown with daisies in her hair, and he was wearing a suit with a daisy in the lapel. He peered closer, his gut churning when he didn't see any evidence of Photoshop.

The door opened, and Lucy appeared, holding a tray of food. "Oh, good. You're up." Her eyes lit with happiness. "That must mean you're feeling a little better. I brought you toast and over-medium eggs just like you like them."

Braxton ignore the food as he flung a hand out, pointing at the wedding photos. "What the hell is this?"

She glanced over at the wall and frowned. "Our wedding pictures?"

"I see that. *But we aren't married.*" He grabbed one of the photos from the wall and threw it on the floor, smashing the glass. "And this room? What are you trying to do, make me think of a time when you weren't insane? Because I have to tell you, it certainly isn't working."

"Brax?" she asked tentatively, her lower lip trembling. "You're scaring me."

"I'm scaring *you*?" he yelled at her. "That's rich when I'm the one you knocked out and brought back to this weird Stepford alternate reality."

"Maybe I should call Dr. Grey. I think that headache is making you agitated." She hurried from the room, but before she could slam the door shut, he put his foot in the way, stopping it and following her into the living room.

He stopped suddenly, taken aback by how eerily familiar it was. The layout of the house wasn't exactly the same, but everything else matched their Savannah house, from the art on the walls to the area rug beneath the shabby secondhand couch and loveseat.

He heard Lucy on the phone talking to someone. Presumably Dr. Grey. Wasn't that the name of the doctor he'd used for his annual checkups way back then? He pressed a hand to his forehead, wondering if he was losing his mind. Had he hit his head and woken up with amnesia? Were all of his memories of the past years just a terrible dream and he really was married to Lucy?

Lily's pretty smile flashed in his mind, and his heart ached to feel her in his arms again.

No. His emotions for Lily were too strong. There was no way he'd dreamed that into existence. He couldn't have, could he? He walked over to the window and peered out at the blue water. This definitely wasn't Savannah. He scanned the area, took in the tall trees, the hydrangeas, and spent rhododendrons, and he knew without a doubt that they were still somewhere near Befana Bay. The view was of the Puget Sound.

"Dr. Grey said to give you one of my calming potions," Lucy said, standing back at the kitchen entrance. "He said since you hit your head last night, you're probably having some strange short-term memory problems."

"Dr. Grey, huh?"

"Yeah. Your doctor," she said. "Remember Dr. Grey?"

"I remember that he had a practice in Savannah, not Washington," he said, his tone empty of all emotion.

"Right. He's in Savannah and we're here in Kingston. He said he'd be available for phone consultations as long as we needed him. We've called him before. Remember when you had that nasty cough and he sent us a healing potion?"

His world began to spin again. Why couldn't he make heads or tails out of what was happening? His life in Befana Bay, his store, Lily, and Dante were crystal clear. Not to mention his memories of moving to Tybee Island after Lucy had cursed him and disappeared. He'd managed an outdoor store there until a hurricane came and destroyed that shop. It was shortly after that when he'd come to Befana Bay and opened his own store, hoping for a fresh start. He hadn't been disappointed. He'd adjusted to not having someone special, and for the most part his life was great, right up until a few days ago when his mother arrived and all hell started breaking loose.

"Braxton." Lucy walked over to him and placed her hand

on his chest. "I know you've had a rough morning. Why don't you just let me take care of you like I always do?"

Take care of him? When had Lucy ever done anything other than for herself? That's when he knew everything was a lie. "Cut the crap, Lucy. Do you really think you're going to gaslight me into thinking that you never cursed me? That you and my mother never teamed up to scam a bunch of innocent people? That's not something someone just forgets overnight."

"Curse you?" she asked, looking shocked. "Why would I ever do that? And I certainly don't scam people. I'm sorry, Braxton, but you're acting crazy. Don't you see how nuts that sounds? And how could I have teamed up with your mother?" Her eyes welled with what he just knew were fake tears. "She died a few years ago, babe. Don't you remember?" She pointed to another picture on a side table that he hadn't seen yet. It was a photo of a tombstone with his mother's name and a death date of over three years ago.

My mother is not dead! he wanted to scream at her, horrified by the lengths she would go to in an attempt to make him think they were actually married and she hadn't made his life a living hell. But he could see her getting agitated as her eyes tinted red. He'd witnessed that once before; it was right before she'd cursed him.

A shadow in the window behind her caught his eye, and for the briefest second, he spotted Niko peering in at him. His friend gave him a slight shake of his head and then disappeared.

Lucy spun, staring in the direction of the window. "Is something out there?"

"Just a hummingbird," he said as he sat in the lumpy chair. Relief crashed through him. He wasn't going insane after all. All he had to do was bide his time until Niko was ready to make his move. Braxton looked up at Lucy and asked, "Why haven't we gotten new furniture?"

The redness in her eyes vanished, and her smile was back. "We were saving our money to buy this house. When you're feeling better, we can go look at some new options. We should be able to swing it soon. I have some orders to fill."

"Potions and spells?" he asked.

She nodded. "You know, energy and skin brightening potions. Those celebrities sure are willing to plunk down the cash just for a little extra glow." She winked at him, appearing relieved he was no longer challenging her.

She walked over to the desk drawer and started searching for something. "I got those brochures for that Hawaiian vacation we talked about."

They had talked about a vacation on the island at one point. Or rather she had. Braxton had never wanted to go. After living in Florida and then Georgia for so many years, he'd been tired of the heat and humidity and hadn't felt the need to vacation in the tropics.

"Where are they?" she mumbled to herself, kneeling on the floor as she searched. It was a rare moment of letting her guard down, and that's when Niko made his move and burst through the back door.

But Lucy was too fast for him. She must have sensed his presence, because the second he shot off a spell to neutralize her, she blocked it with one of her own and then shot two more back at him and his partner.

No. Not his partner.

Lily.

Braxton lost all control and tackled Lucy. The two of them went down in a heap of limbs, both grappling for purchase. Braxton, who'd had the element of surprise, rolled her over and clasped his hands around her neck. Her fingers clawed at his grip, but he was stronger. She might wield magic, but he had brute strength. All he had to do was make her pass out, and then they could contain her.

But Lucy was too powerful. Her eyes flashed red and a second later, a bolt of heat slammed into his chest, sending him flying into the nearest wall.

"No!" he heard Lily cry as he landed on the hardwood with a *thunk.*

CHAPTER 23

"GET AWAY FROM US," Lucy warned Lily, standing over Braxton like a shield. "I swear to the goddess that if you and that asshole agent don't leave right now, I'll kill him. I'll do it. I will."

"And spend the rest of your life locked up in prison?" Niko asked from behind Lily. They'd busted in the back door and were now inside the small house that sat high on the hillside so that it had a view of the Sound. It had taken them a few hours for the wolf to lead them to the house, and then they'd spent time staking it out, determining where Braxton was and what kind of protections Lucy had used.

Niko and Lily had disabled more than a handful of magical traps before they'd even been able to look in a window. But when they finally did, they'd realized that Lucy was even more insane than they'd previously assumed. Niko said it was a byproduct of siphoning other witches' magic. It would slowly make one go insane. Lucy had apparently spent a number of years stealing magic. Katerina was just her latest victim.

"I'll die before I go to that hellhole," she spat. "If I'm lucky, I'll take both of you with me."

"Fat chance," Lily said with a dismissive snort. She could feel the power radiating off the other witch and knew she would be a challenge, but Lily had something more powerful on her side.

Love.

Every witch knew that love always trumped greed and hatred, and those were the two emotions that ruled Lucy.

"Watch me!" Lucy unleashed a torrent of magic on Lily, but the Befana witch was more than ready for her stream of toxic magic.

Lily instantly put up a magical reflective shield that sent Lucy's magic rebounding. The magic slammed into the far wall, causing a loud crash as it crumbled.

"My house!" Lucy cried.

"If you're dead, you won't need it," Lily reasoned and sent her own stream of magic at the crazy witch.

The two were locked in a duel, each of them pouring everything they had into the fight.

Out of the corner of her eye, Lily spotted Niko running over to Braxton to help him out of the fray. Lily was grateful and made a mental note to thank him later. She could handle Lucy. As long as Braxton was safe, that was all she needed to know.

"He's mine! He's bound to me!" Lucy called. "He'll never be yours."

"He already is." Lily's voice was calm as she poured all of her concentration into the magic she needed to take down Braxton's ex. One way or another, she was leaving that house with Braxton, preferably with the curse broken.

The two stayed locked like that for what seemed like hours but was probably only minutes, while Niko tried to get Braxton out of the house and out of the fray. But Braxton had come around and was refusing to go. He wasn't leaving Lily. Not while she was battling Lucy.

Frustrated, Niko told him he'd better take care of himself and then got to work on making a holding circle. It was part of the plan. Lily would attack Lucy and force her into the circle, where she'd be held until a team from the Magical Task Force could arrive to take her away.

Lily wished Braxton would stay out of the fray, but she couldn't blame him. If the situation was reversed, she wouldn't leave either. Her hands were tired from pouring magic out at an unprecedented rate, but she didn't let up. In fact, she concentrated harder and sent Lucy stumbling back a few paces. She was almost there. Just a few more steps and they'd have her. The assault worked to break Lucy's concentration, and she caught herself as she was going down.

Lily took full advantage and sent a bolt of power that was intended to knock her right into the circle. But just before the assault hit her, a photo frame came out of nowhere, and Lucy dodged to the right. The silver frame barely grazed Lucy, but the magical bolt missed and put a giant crater in the wall.

Off to the side of her, Lily heard Braxton curse and she assumed he was the one who threw the picture frame.

Lucy let out a cry of frustration and sent two bolts of magic, one with each hand, though she didn't send them toward Lily. They hit their intended targets. Brax and Niko went down in a tangle of limbs.

"You're going to pay for that!" Lily cried and prayed that Braxton and Niko were okay. They had to be. She'd never survive it if she lost Braxton now. She took a step forward, her entire body vibrating with rage. Lucy's eyes were bloodshot, and she looked as deranged as Lily felt. With her two allies out of commission, Lily poured everything she had into defeating Lucy.

Sweat poured down her face, and her limbs started to tremble. She wasn't sure how long she could keep this up, but she'd go as long as needed in order to defeat this woman who'd reigned terror on too many people to count.

Good had to win over evil. She believed that with all her soul.

She pictured Braxton's smiling face when they were out on their hike and felt a renewal of energy. Something soft brushed against her skin, and she realized the white wolf was there, giving her strength. *Thank you*, she mouthed to the creature.

Then with every bit of determination she could muster, she took a step forward and sent one last bolt of magic right at Lucy's chest.

The other witch froze in place, her magic vanishing from the dust-filled air. Lucy fell backward, right into the circle Niko had formed before she'd taken him down.

Silence filled the small house as Lily walked over to the body lying there. As she peered over the other witch, the air felt thick with magic, and suddenly all the magical energy that Lucy had consumed over the years rushed into Lily, sending her to her knees as she retched from the awful intrusion of the magic she hadn't asked for.

Her vision blurred, and the last thing she heard before she passed out was Braxton's voice.

"Lily? Lily? I've got you. Don't worry. I've got you."

You did well. Your mother would be very proud of you, a strange voice said in Lily's head.

Lily blinked up at the familiar ceiling, her limbs as heavy as molasses. She glanced around and recognized her old room at her grandmother's house and thanked the gods that she was still alive.

You'll be okay as long as you don't cast any magic, the voice added.

"Ever?" Lily asked out loud, though she had no idea who she was talking to.

No. Just until the coven is able to release the magic.

"Who are you?" she asked, afraid she was harboring someone else's soul. Why else would someone be talking in her head?

Something cool and wet nudged her hand and she glanced down to see the white wolf was sitting next to her bed, apparently keeping an eye on her. "You're the one talking to me? How?"

Yes. Your mother sent me to watch over you. You can hear me for the time being because of the extra power you carry.

"What?" she gasped out. "When? How?" Lily's brain was a jumble of confusion. Was she hallucinating this?

There was a faint chuckle in the back of her mind before the wolf explained. *When your sister Sage battled the witches of Crystal Point in the spring, your mother came to me and said that her girls were coming into their power, and she needed me to watch over you all. I've been doing that ever since. Think of me as a guardian angel of sorts.*

"Mom is still watching over us?" Lily asked, tears falling silently down her temples.

Always.

"That's… I don't know what to say." Her emotions had gotten the better of her. "Thank you."

You're welcome, Lily. The wolf turned to go, but when he reached the doorway, he turned back again. *Remember, no magic until the coven siphons the excess off. If you don't wait, you'll be cursed with stolen power for the rest of your days.*

"I'll remember," she promised and was sad to see the wolf go.

Just call to me in your mind if you need me again. I'll be there.

A weight that had seemed to be on Lily's chest lifted, and she smiled softly to herself, knowing for the first time that even though her mother had passed, she'd never really be gone for good.

"You're awake," Bethany said as she walked into the room, smiling softly.

"Where's Braxton?" Lily asked immediately.

"He's here," her grandmother said patiently. "The healer

is with him now. He'll be fine. Lucy shot him up with some potion that was meant to make him more pliable to her gaslighting, but it appears he was stronger than she anticipated. Once they neutralize it, he'll be as good as new."

"What about the curse? If Lucy lost her magic, how can she reverse it?" Lily tried to sit up and found she could barely move. Her limbs were just too heavy.

"Relax, love. The curse is broken. Braxton is no longer tied to her," Bethany soothed. "All of her curses died the moment her collected power drained into you."

Lily laid back on the pillow and said a silent thank you to the universe on Braxton's behalf that Lucy was now out of his life. But dread still plagued her. "Does this mean he's tied to me now?"

"No. Why would he be?" Bethany seemed confused.

"Because Lucy's power drained into me for some reason."

Recognition dawned in her grandmother's eyes. "I see what you're getting at. But no, that's not how it works. The moment her magic left her body, those curses failed to exist. The magic you are harboring is the stolen power from other witches. We need to drain it from you so it doesn't harm your soul. The coven is on their way."

"Could I have stopped it?" Lily asked.

"No, sweetheart. That power needed somewhere to go once Lucy was trapped in the binding circle. You were the only one there to receive it. There was nothing you could have done to stop it. You did not invite this. Don't worry."

"That's a relief."

"I bet it is," she said with a soft chuckle.

Ten minutes later, Serena, Jacinda, and the rest of the coven had gathered around Lily's bed and were all holding hands as they slowly eased the excess power into the ether. With each second that ticked by, Lily felt her soul get lighter and lighter until finally all she felt was peace.

"That went rather well," Bethany said.

The door burst open, and Katerina stumbled in. Her eyes were wild, and there was an air of desperation streaming off her. "I'm here to get my power back."

The coven witches glanced at each other, their eyebrows raised.

Bethany cleared her throat. "I'm sorry, Katerina, it's too late."

Braxton's mother stared blankly at her as if she hadn't heard what she said. "No. You're going to get me my powers back. I am *not* leaving here until someone fixes what that psycho did to me."

Niko walked in right after her and said, "That's not going to happen."

She spun and poked him in the chest with her index finger. "I've had just about enough of you. I didn't deserve to be harassed for all those years. It's not my fault people are so gullible they'll buy anything if they think it will make them look even five minutes younger."

"That's not why you were of interest to the Magical Task Force, and you know it, Katerina," he said, his eyes narrowed. "Think of it as a blessing that you didn't get your powers back. Now you're not a threat to society. You'll likely just get some probation and you can go on living your life. If you *had* gotten them back, you'd be looking at a decade or more in prison. I suggest you leave Lily and her family alone now. They can't help you."

Katerina glared at everyone. "You all think you're so high and mighty. You'd never last without your powers either. I don't care what you say," she added when she focused on Niko again. "I'm not living a life without my magic. I'll get it back one way or another." Then she stormed out, nearly splintering the door when it slammed against the wall.

"Do you think she'll be successful?" Lily asked.

All the coven witches shook their heads, but Niko shrugged. "Maybe. If she finds someone willing to siphon power for her. If she does, she'll end up in prison. The MTF isn't going to stop keeping tabs on her just because she's been neutralized. You can't live that kind of life for so long without consequences."

Niko patted Lily's shoulder. "I'm glad you're all right. You're one hell of a witch."

"Thanks." She gave him a small smile. "You're not so bad yourself."

CHAPTER 24

BRAXTON HELD Lily's hand in both of his as they sat in his living room with Niko and Dante. It had been a few days since the battle with Lucy, and everyone had fully recovered. At least everyone except Lucy, who was in the paranormal prison hospital recovering from years of destruction to her soul from harboring so many stolen energies.

"Is she even fit to stand trial?" Lily asked Niko. "That power that she stole was brutal. I don't know how she lived like that day in and day out."

"She'll stand trial," he said. "She's not so far gone that any judge will believe that she's mentally insane. A psychopath, maybe, but she knew what she was doing then, and she knows what she did now. Power addiction is a hell of a drug."

"How long have you been tracking her?" Braxton asked.

He'd been dying to get the details of Niko's life ever since they'd left Bethany Befana's house two days ago, but Niko had been gone, dealing with paperwork and procedural red tape after the capture of one of the Magical Task Force's top ten most wanted.

"About three years." He gave them a sheepish smile. "But I got thrown off the case about six months ago when someone found out my connection to you. They said I was making the case too personal."

"Weren't you?" Lily asked with a knowing smile.

"Sure. But it's not like I couldn't do my job. I had been tracking Lucy for months, and one day, she got the better of me and nearly put me in a magical coma. If it hadn't been for a stray wolf running in her path, she would have."

"A wolf?" Braxton and Lily shared a knowing look. She'd told him about her conversation with the guardian angel that had helped them find him at the other house Lucy had rented.

"It was gray, not white, so don't go thinking the two are connected," Niko said.

"Okay," Braxton said. "If you say so."

"Anyway, they said they were taking me off the case. I was furious. I was this close to finally nailing Lucy to the wall, so I took a little time off and tracked her on my personal time. They don't love that, but since I brought her in, they've decided to overlook it."

Dante leaned forward with his hands clasped together. "All this time you've been an agent with the Magical Task Force. Why didn't you tell us?"

It was a question Braxton was dying to have answered as well.

"Because my main case was tracking Katerina, and I couldn't afford to have either of you involved, considering our history. And I just didn't think that would be possible. I know there was no love lost between you and your mother, but family does strange things when they find out a relative is being pursued by law enforcement. It was just too risky."

Braxton wanted to say that he'd have helped in any way he could, but he didn't know what he would have done if faced with having to choose between his mother or helping Niko. He hadn't wanted her to move in, but he'd let her do it with the promise that she'd break the curse. He knew now that she never intended to do any such thing. She only wanted her power back, and she knew Lucy was in the area. He imagined that if it had been convenient to break the curse, or if it had been some sort of side benefit to her, she wouldn't have cared. But to put the effort in to help him? No, that was never in the cards.

"Makes sense," Dante said.

Braxton nodded his agreement.

"What are you going to do now?" Lily asked him. "Do you head back to Florida?"

"No. Not likely. I thought I'd stick around here for a while." His eyes sparkled with mischief.

"On leave or…" Lily asked.

"The MTF is letting me pick my field office. There's one about twenty miles south of here. I thought I'd give living in the Pacific Northwest a try. Maybe take out that girl I have my eye on."

Lily gave him a skeptical look. "If you're talking about my sister, she doesn't date people in law enforcement."

"Sure she does," he said easily. "She already has. She just didn't realize it at the time."

Lily shook her head. "She has trust issues. Let's just leave it at that."

Niko's amusement fled as he held Lily's gaze. "What does that mean?"

"You'll have to talk to her about it. I'm just warning you that now that she knows what you really do, don't be surprised if she bows out of whatever you two had going on."

He let out a huff and stood. "Well, I guess we'll just have to wait and see." He pulled his baseball cap on. "I've got to go see about that auction. Wish me luck."

Lily gasped. "You really are interested in buying that blue house?"

"Yep. You see, it's not *all* cloak and dagger and lies." He winked at her and then waved to his friends. "See you for beers later?"

"Not me. Lily and I have plans," Braxton said, eyeing Lily, who flushed pink.

"I'll be there," Dante said then laughed. "If you two come back here, be sure to put a sock on the doorknob. I don't want to interrupt anything."

Lily flushed a darker red as she shook her head.

Braxton just laughed. "Will do."

BRAXTON WRAPPED his arm around Lily as they strolled along the waterfront. The full moon was out, and a pair of orcas were milling around in the bay. They'd had dinner at The Salt Circle and were now just enjoying everything Befana Bay had to offer.

Lily pointed out an older man who had a dog dressed in a pink outfit as she trotted along next to him. "I'm going to get a little dog someday."

"Yeah? What kind?"

"A Lhasa apso. Gran had one when we were kids, and that dog was so affectionate with her but very territorial and mean to most everyone else. She was the best guard dog we ever had."

He laughed. "Sounds reasonable after the last few weeks. Maybe I'll get one, too."

She chuckled. "Nah, we'll get one together. Her name has to be Rizzo though. Caustic on the outside, but loveable mush on the inside."

"You're on." His heart was full. Ever since the curse had been lifted, his life had been calm. There weren't any more women doing crazy things to get his attention. He and Lily had started to talk about a life together in the future instead of always avoiding the topic. It was the first time in his life when he woke up excited to see what each day would bring him.

"Aw, I can't wait to have a puppy," she said excitedly. "Is tomorrow too early to start looking?"

He laughed. "Nope."

"Good."

They were silent for a bit until Braxton said, "Thank you."

She leaned into him, her hand warm in his. "For what?"

"Everything. You gave me my life back." He paused and lifted his hand, burying it in her hair. "There are no words to express just how grateful I am for the gift you've given me. The only thing I can do is show you every day just how much I appreciate you."

She closed her eyes and leaned into his touch. When she opened them and met his gaze, a small smile claimed her lips. "You can't give me that much credit. I did it for me just as much as I did it for you."

"What does that mean?" he asked, caressing her cheek.

"It means I was getting tired of saying goodnight to you at my door. I wanted to be with you in all the ways that matter, but with that curse hanging between us..." She shrugged. "I'm hoping tomorrow is the morning I'll finally wake up with you in my bed."

Braxton was breathless as he leaned in and whispered, "Consider it done." He claimed her lips, kissing her with a passion that seemed to come straight from his soul. Both of his hands were in her hair, and he pressed her up against the railing as her soft body arched into him.

He tasted her over and over and over again, until finally she pulled away and said, "Take me home, Brax."

He grabbed her hand, and together they hurried up the hill to her house. The moment they were inside, he swept her up into his arms and carried her upstairs.

Lily giggled as he took two stairs at a time. "In a hurry?"

"You bet your ass."

She didn't waste any time either. Before he even got her to the top of the stairs, she was already unbuttoning his shirt. When they made it to her bedroom, they were hurried and impatient, pulling each other's clothes off.

And then they fell into bed, lost in each other. Finally showing one another just how deeply in love they were.

CHAPTER 25

INDIGO EASTON LOOKED out at all the people milling around the Midsummer Festival and felt a surge of pride for her sister and Braxton. She was well aware that Cassandra had majorly dropped the ball on planning the event, but no one would be the wiser. Everything had gone as smooth as silk, and it appeared that not only was everyone having a great time, but her grandmother had raised quite a bit of money for the youth witch summer program she was so passionate about.

The booth Indigo was manning wasn't doing too shabby either. To be fair, Brooms that Vroom always did well at witch festivals, but this was something else. They'd nearly sold out of the junior brooms, and all the rentals she'd allocated for the weekend had been reserved. She'd need to do something nice for Lily as a thank you. Without her, the shop wouldn't have gotten this influx of cash, and Indigo wouldn't be mentally planning the mini kitchen remodel she'd dreamed of. She was dying for some quartz countertops and a new refrigerator.

"Hey, sis," Prim said as she handed Indigo an iced latte. "Need a break?"

"You're a goddess," she said as she took the drink. "It's been crazy busy here."

Prim glanced around at the picked-over inventory and said, "I can see that. The yarn tent isn't doing too terrible either. This morning was crazy when we released the special edition witchery skeins, but it's slowed down now, and Vivian's got it handled."

"Are you sure you have time to man my booth for a few minutes?" Indigo asked, not wanting to overload her sister. Prim was always the one going out of her way to help everyone else. She didn't want to take advantage.

"Sure. When you get back, I'll let Vivian head out to enjoy the festival. Not many people are interested in fiber when it's pushing eighty-five degrees." Prim gave her sister a little nudge. "Go on. Check it out. I'll text you if I need anything."

Indigo gave her sister a quick hug and kissed her on top of the head. "You're the best."

"I know." Prim gave her a cheeky grin and then turned to start straightening a row of brooms that Indigo had just straightened ten minutes ago.

With an amused laugh, Indigo headed for the corn hole competition and watched as August and Sage played a friendly match. When her sister annihilated him, Indigo pumped her fist into the air and let out a whoop of approval. Sage bowed and then hugged August as they both laughed.

Lily strolled up and leaned against the railing. "Interested in getting your butt kicked?"

Indigo chuckled. "Not particularly."

"How about gossiping about that sexy guy staring at you?" she asked as she jerked her head toward Niko and then pumped her eyebrows suggestively.

"Also not interested." Indigo turned her back on Niko so she wouldn't encourage him staring at her.

"He's a good guy," Lily said as if Indigo didn't already know that.

"That's not the problem, and you know it."

Lily gave her a sympathetic smile. "Isn't it though?"

Indigo ground her teeth together. "I really don't want to talk about this. It's too nice a day to dwell on things we can't change. Besides, we should be talking about you and Braxton. I heard you had an official date the other night. How'd it go?"

Lily turned and scanned the crowd until she found Braxton, who was helping at the kayak rentals. "It was perfect," she said with a sigh. "Just perfect."

"Good goddess. That sounds like wedding bells and babies are in your future," Indigo said, sounding horrified.

"Wedding bells, maybe. I wouldn't say no. But babies?" She grimaced at her sister. "No. But I am scouting out a puppy. That's enough baby for me."

Indigo wasn't surprised that Lily wasn't thinking about

having kids. Prim was the only one who seemed to really have a desire for a family. For the rest of them, babies didn't seem to be in the cards. At least not any time soon.

And especially not for Indigo. She'd thought that was her future once. But then everything had gone to hell with the person she thought she was going to marry. And now, she was content to run her shop and go on the occasional date, but nothing serious.

"Uh-oh. Here he comes," Lily said and then ran off, giving her sister a finger wave.

She scowled at Lily, mentally cursing her for abandoning her in her time of need. Not that she needed Lily exactly, but she could've used a buffer. Ever since she'd learned that Niko was law enforcement, she'd done her best to keep her distance.

"You were right," Niko said.

"Of course I was," Indigo said with a cheeky smile. "About what this time?"

He laughed and pulled out the book she'd given him. "Cozy mystery, at least the kind written by Jana DeLeon, is excellent. Funny *and* a well-crafted mystery. I've already purchased the next book in the series."

"I won't say I told you so, but..." She winked at him, hating that she enjoyed bantering with him so much.

"You told me so." His eyes were full of humor when he said, "Now I owe you that romantic dinner. Are you free later this week?"

"I really don't—"

"You're not going to cheat me out of paying up on my bet, are you?"

She peered at him and had to give him credit. He was working hard for this date. She knew that Lily had warned him that she didn't date law enforcement, and she had good reasons for that policy. Ones she hadn't forgotten. But how could she resist a man who had her same taste in books? "No. I guess not. But this date better include a trip to the bookstore."

His lips turned up into a sexy half-smile. "Dinner, bookstore, and a moonlit stroll. How's Wednesday sound?"

It was her day off, a fact he probably knew all too well.

"I'll even throw in a horseback ride on the beach," he teased, making her laugh.

When they'd met in Florida, the one thing she said she never wanted to do was horseback riding on the beach. She'd said it was the epitome of cheese. He'd countered that cheese was what made the world go around, and when she lost a bet to him, he'd taken her on a midnight horseback ride on the beach. Unfortunately, her horse decided to buck her off into the waves, and he'd had to concede that it was, in fact, the most unromantic date to ever exist.

But then he'd taken her back to her hotel. And after one night in bed together, the horseback ride had been utterly forgotten.

"Skip the horseback ride. Dinner, bookstore, and a midnight kayak ride," she said. "That's a lot more romantic than a stroll."

"You're on." He reached out and took her hand in his, held it for a beat longer than necessary, and then slowly let it drop before he walked away.

Indigo watched him and pressed her hand to her stomach, trying and failing to calm the butterflies.

"Did you just say yes to a date with Niko?" Lily asked, appearing out of nowhere.

Indigo nodded and hung her head. What had she just done?

DEANNA'S BOOK LIST

Witches of Keating Hollow:
Soul of the Witch
Heart of the Witch
Spirit of the Witch
Dreams of the Witch
Courage of the Witch
Love of the Witch
Power of the Witch
Essence of the Witch
Muse of the Witch
Vision of the Witch
Waking of the Witch
Honor of the Witch
Promise of the Witch
Return of the Witch
Fortune of the Witch
Song of the Witch

Keating Hollow Happily Ever Afters:
Gift of the Witch
Wisdom of the Witch
Light of the Witch

Witches of Befana Bay:
The Witch's Silver Lining
The Witch's Secret Love
The Witch's Lost Spell

Witches of Christmas Grove:
A Witch For Mr. Holiday
A Witch For Mr. Christmas
A Witch For Mr. Winter
A Witch For Mr. Mistletoe
A Witch For Mr. Frost
A Witch For Mr. Garland

Premonition Pointe Novels:
Witching For Grace
Witching For Hope
Witching For Joy
Witching For Clarity
Witching For Moxie
Witching For Kismet

Miss Matched Midlife Dating Agency:
Star-crossed Witch
Honor-bound Witch

Outmatched Witch
Moonstruck Witch
Rainmaker Witch

Jade Calhoun Novels:
Haunted on Bourbon Street
Witches of Bourbon Street
Demons of Bourbon Street
Angels of Bourbon Street
Shadows of Bourbon Street
Incubus of Bourbon Street
Bewitched on Bourbon Street
Hexed on Bourbon Street
Dragons of Bourbon Street

Pyper Rayne Novels:
Spirits, Stilettos, and a Silver Bustier
Spirits, Rock Stars, and a Midnight Chocolate Bar
Spirits, Beignets, and a Bayou Biker Gang
Spirits, Diamonds, and a Drive-thru Daiquiri Stand
Spirits, Spells, and Wedding Bells

Ida May Chronicles:
Witched To Death
Witch, Please
Stop Your Witchin'

Crescent City Fae Novels:
Influential Magic

Irresistible Magic
Intoxicating Magic

Last Witch Standing:
Bewitched by Moonlight
Soulless at Sunset
Bloodlust By Midnight
Bitten At Daybreak

Witch Island Brides:
The Wolf's New Year Bride
The Vampire's Last Dance
The Warlock's Enchanted Kiss
The Shifter's First Bite

Destiny Novels:
Defining Destiny
Accepting Fate

Wolves of the Rising Sun:
Jace
Aiden
Luc
Craved
Silas
Darien
Wren

Black Bear Outlaws:
Cyrus

Chase

Cole

Bayou Springs Alien Mail Order Brides:

Zeke

Gunn

Echo

ABOUT THE AUTHOR

New York Times and USA Today bestselling author, Deanna Chase, is a native Californian, transplanted to the slower paced lifestyle of southeastern Louisiana. When she isn't writing, she is often goofing off with her husband in New Orleans or playing with her two shih tzu dogs. For more information and updates on newest releases visit her website at deannachase.com.

www.ingramcontent.com/pod-product-compliance
Lightning Source LLC
Chambersburg PA
CBHW020404210626
46016CD00006DB/2113